FAR WEST

FAR WEST

Stories

Ron Tanner

ELIXIR PRESS
DENVER, COLORADO

Book design by Steven Seighman

Library of Congress Cataloging-in-Publication Data

Names: Tanner, Ron, 1953- author.
Title: Far west : stories / Ron Tanner.
Description: First edition. | Denver, Colorado : Elixir Press,
2022. |
Summary: "Winner of the Elixir Press Fiction Award.
Short stories"--
Provided by publisher.
Identifiers: LCCN 2021029090 | ISBN 9781932418774
(paperback)
Subjects: GSAFD: Short stories. | LCGFT: Short stories.
Classification: LCC PS3620.A69 F37 2022 | DDC
813/.6--dc23
LC record available at https://lccn.loc.gov/2021029090

ISBN: 978-1-932-41877-4

First edition: 2022

10   9   8   7   6   5   4   3   2   1

Beyond the glittering street was darkness,
and beyond the darkness the West.

—JACK KEROUAC

It has been observed that all Americans need a frontier.

—SALMAN RUSHDIE

To Jo Anderson and John Coinman,
living the dream in America's west.

TABLE OF CONTENTS

Introduction   1

1. Winnemucca   5
2. Boom, Like That!   22
3. Jackpot   39
4. Six Blind Cats   55
5. Save the Poor Dumb Creatures   62
6. Tarzan (Again)   74
7. Samuel's Secret   89
8. Far West   113
9. Diversity!   127
10. Wheels   152

Acknowledgments   173

INTRODUCTION

The characters in Ron Tanner's collection, Far West, are people readers can relate to not only with sympathy, but admiration. While many are disappointed dreamers, they don't tolerate pretense. These people struggle with lifting veils of complacency and false beauty and while the process is painful, I applaud their demand for authenticity over easy falsehoods.

Many of the stories investigate the American West, examining themes like independence, freedom, and space with a lens of honesty and grit. In "Winnemucca," for instance, Rainy is the drummer for an all-girl country band touring Nevada. She hits the jackpot at the slot machine then nearly loses it all to sweet-talking Levon Little, who suggests they run away together so he can show her "the "mountains" where there are "aspen, canyons and waterfalls." And here it is, the classic fantasy of the West—escape to the mountains and run free. Even Rainy, a profound realist, pauses to consider. Then Little announces he's going to take the cash anyway, so she might as well come with him.

Rainy reappears in the collection's final story, "Wheels." She travels home to California after her father has suffered a stroke. Though she clearly loves her parents, Rainy sees them as "two oldish people with dwindling prospects and a daughter who couldn't leave them and their Valley fast enough." The strangeness of returning home as an adult compounds the guilt she feels over refusing to stay longer. In fact, she feels guilty for leaving in the first place, indeed, for growing up:

> "I'll be back," I promised. I realized I kept saying this every time I saw them. Ten years earlier I had left in the same van, in almost the same way. It was eerie. Is this what children do, haunt their parents?

For all the heavy thematic content, Tanner's stories are not without humor. The situations themselves are often funny. The unnamed narrator of "Jackpot," for instance, is a gambling addict banned from Reno casinos for attempting to rig slot machines. Now he's hired to drive for Tiny Britten, an mechanical engineer who hopes to see wild mustangs on the high desert. Her husband Mars is a man who likes to sun himself to the point of delirium. The narrator's description of the landscape sums up the no-nonsense honesty of the collection, a tone that helps it realize its awareness of the forever unattained:

> Nevada can be pretty. But not here. We were in the stone-hard heart of the state. It's high desert—not your white-sand-and-big-cacti cliché but packed dirt studded with

sagebrush as far as you can see, each bush the size of a basketball. From a distance they make the land look leprous. The mountains are nothing more than naked rock, so barren they made me wonder if hell could look worse. Nobody wanted this land. That's why it was wide open.

The settings in these tales are insistent; many of the plots hinge on where they take place. The Marshall Islands, for instance, is the setting for two stories featuring recurring teen characters, Nora, an American who lives on the island of Kwajalein, and Jeton, a native Micronesian from Ebeye, who meet at a soccer game between their schools. In "Boom! Like that!" Jeton compares the islands, observing that their differences begin with the streets. On Kwajalein "they are wide and paved and bright with electric light. The houses are neat, they all look alike, the yards are clear of motorbikes, scrap wood, trash, and chickens, and everything everywhere is green." But Jeton prefers Ebeye with its "haphazard houses and the sandy streets that curl and twist like vines," a place where "animals . . . run freely and the children playing everywhere you turn and the cooking smells and the women singing and the laundry flagging from the lines over the dirt yards—all of this feels good."

Jeton, like most characters in Tanner's collection, seeks authenticity even as he runs from it. The work speaks directly to this push and pull, a resistance to the "white-sand-and-big-cacti cliché," towards the call of places that are gritty and dirty and flawed, but real, places that "feel good."

The supermodels in "Save the Poor Dumb Creatures" travel to exotic, poverty-stricken beach locales and hand out steaks to the locals to stop them from taking sea turtle eggs. Even Tarzan engages in myth busting. In "Tarzan, Again," he has been abandoned by Jane and is raising "Boy," their son, in Los Angeles. Tarzan tries to console Boy after Cheetah's violent death. He "wants to believe in all good things for Boy's benefit," but after what he's lived through, he can't quite.

Ultimately Tanner's stories are a delight because he is a masterful writer. Full of sharp dialogue that either advances the plot or sharpens the characters, or both, the stories are a terrific combination of poignant, absurd and profound. They present landscapes that are more complex than they appear. Tanner's work promotes an intolerance for cliché and over simplicity and as such, his stories are unforgettable.

—*Christy Stillwell, Contest Judge*

WINNEMUCCA

I pounded on Nancy's door for several minutes before I tried the knob. The door was unlocked. As I entered, a cold wind blew in behind me, pushing my skirt tight between my legs. I could smell creosote and sage. I pictured tumbleweeds rolling and bouncing, bullied by the wind.

I'd come to tell Nancy that Pepper was MIA. I'd just seen her fiddle for sale in the local pawnshop. I made a habit of checking the pawnshops because Pepper was always hocking something.

Without a fiddle, we didn't sound much like a country band. We had been gigging two weeks at Winnemucca's Te-Moak Casino. Nancy joked that Winnemucca was Indian for "where the fuck are we?" I didn't like being on the road. I had tried to quit it six months back, but here I was again, halfway across Nevada. When I'd left Kai in Berkeley, he said, "Why do you want to live this way?" All I could do was shrug, then kiss him hard on the mouth, as if that would hold him.

Nancy was sprawled on her stomach across the bed, like she had landed there after falling from a great height, white-blonde hair fanned neatly across her bare back. She had her jeans on but no shoes.

"Nancy?"

Her room smelled of baby powder and puke. A tinge of mildew too. The puke smell could have been anything. It didn't mean she was bulimic or drinking, problems that had dogged her for years. She was thirty-five, still holding tight to the look of a late twenty-something.

The wind kicked up a dust devil outside the uncurtained window. I could see blue-gray mountains in the distance. This was high desert but not the pretty kind you'd find in Arizona or New Mexico. Nevada landscape in these parts was as underfed and scrubby as a coyote.

I stepped closer, then grabbed the cool heel of Nancy's left foot.

Nancy jerked awake and rolled over so quickly, I jumped back.

"Jesus, girl!"

Her face was swollen from sleep, a strand of too-blond hair stuck to her lower lip. A big block of mid-day sunlight fell through the open door behind me and lit up the mess of Nancy's room.

"You wouldn't answer," I said. "I was *pounding*."

"Sure, pounding," she said. "That's what drummers do."

"You all right?"

"I was writing." She glanced around for something lost, then pulled a t-shirt from the tangle of sheets. "You want to hear it?"

"We don't have time," I said.

Nancy was no song writer, but that didn't stop her from trying. Nearly every musician I knew was the same. Writing songs was like playing the slots. Maybe you'd get lucky.

"Everyone has time for a love song," she said.

"Pepper hocked her fiddle."

Nancy grimaced as she squirmed into her t-shirt. "She's such an asshole."

Other times, Pepper had hocked her turquoise-studded belt, her ten-gallon hat, her silver bangles or her diamond ear stud, even her back-up bow, but never her fiddle.

I used to think: *if I was band leader I'd never hire a flake.* But, now twenty-nine, I'd come to realize that most people are flaky. Pepper was a good player. She remembered the arrangements. She didn't have attitude on stage. But we were always running after her off-stage. Nobody has it all, that's the thing. No matter who you are, there's going to be a hole in your program. So it was with Kai. I loved him to death, but he was killing me. I was on the road because he couldn't pay the rent. He knew that. And yet he blamed me for going on the road.

"You've gone on like this too long," my mother told me on the phone that morning. "But it's not too late." Ten years before, when I'd refused a scholarship to the College of the Sequoias, I had crushed her dream. Unlike Mark, my older brother, I had no patience for classrooms. I'd never been able to keep my hands still.

"We're in a Recession?" she said. "And all you know how to do is drum?"

I knew plenty: how to tune up my antique VW van, how to make a killer cauliflower casserole, how to housebreak a basset hound, how to run 10 miles without chok-ing, how to repair my wardrobe with needle and thread, how to build a bookcase with reclaimed pallet wood, how to speak enough Spanish to order the really good food from a taco truck, how to scour a flea market for collect-ible silver spoons.

See? Plenty.

Still, I held my hot, little phone to my ear and took it in, as I'd always taken it from Mom: "Think about it, Rainy—who's gonna hire you?"

Nancy would hire me.

I'd been in Nancy's road bands off and on for five years.

I said to Nancy: "You know it's the slots."

"Oh, fuck me." Nancy pulled on her boots.

Nancy dry-smoked a generic cigarette in the passenger seat as I drove my VW bus to main street. "Downtown" was hardly more than a scatter of buildings hunkered by a shallow river. Across the river, Winnemucca Mountain rose from the scrubby desert. Treeless and craggy, blemished with white patches of snow, it was probably bigger than it looked. On the other side was the Sonora Range, huge and intimidating.

I-80 sluices straight through Winnemucca, population 7, 396. The flashiest part was casino row, a short stretch of neon enticements for fast food, gas, and gambling. There were nine casinos. By the time we got to the last one, it was 4:30. We were due on stage at 7:00. "Fuck," said Nancy for the millionth time. "Fuck, fuck, fuck."

When we found Pepper, she was with a man named Levon Little. He raised his Stetson off his head when Pepper introduced us. He was cowboy-lanky but pale as cake flour, with black hair that kept falling over one eye. His eyes were a dewy blue-gray and could have belonged to a kindergarten teacher. He said he was a chef at Te-Moak, though I'd never seen him.

Pepper wouldn't stop playing her machine, even as we talked. Her fingers were black from coins. She was down to a bucket of nickels. Pepper looked sixteen, even though she was twenty-six. She had straight black hair down to her waist and a wide doll-like face. Everywhere she went, there was a man in her wake. It didn't matter that back in Berkeley she was married and had a seven-year-old daughter.

"Gig starts in two hours," Nancy said. She was staring at the back of Pepper's pretty head.

"Right!" Pepper said, yanking the slot arm. She was fond of the old machines, which were easy to find in small towns like Winnemucca.

Nancy turned to Levon and said, "Why'd you let her hock her fiddle?"

Levon blinked in confusion. "I just got here!"

I said, "Pepper, we've got to go get your fiddle."

She smiled sweetly at me. "Would you do that?"

"You've got to go with us," I said.

"I can't leave my machine," she said. "It's about to burp."

"Fuck me!" Nancy said.

I saw Levon look at her with interest. Nancy turned to him and said, "Not talking to you, cowboy."

"I'm a chef," he said.

9

Nancy pulled Pepper's free arm. "Ouch!" Pepper said.

"Come the fuck *on!*" Nancy said.

I said, "Give Pepper three more pulls, Nancy, then we'll go."

"Why three?" Nancy said.

"It's an even number," I joked.

Levon wagged a long finger at me.

I turned to him: "Did you say you were a *chef*?"

He nodded yes.

Pepper had a very fluid motion: coin-to-slot, pull-the-arm, wait-for-the-spin, then-coin-to-slot, and so on.

"I'm not going anywhere," she said.

I pulled out my cell and dialed her house in Berkeley. I said, "I'm calling Tiffany." Her daughter.

Stubb, her husband, answered. "What?"

"It's Stubb," I said.

"I don't want to talk to Stubb," she said.

"He wants to talk to you," I said. In my ear, Stubb said, "No, I don't. Is she stepping off again?"

Nancy said to Levon: "You don't want to get mixed up in this."

Levon said, "I'm not mixed up in anything." Then he winked at me like we shared a secret. I felt my ear burning where the phone was. I thought of microwaves coursing through my head. This was autumn, 2008. Nobody had smart phones yet.

"I'm not leaving this machine," Pepper said.

Suddenly Stubb was weeping in my ear. "She's cheating on me again, isn't she?" I hated myself for pulling him into this. A band is like a family in all the worst ways.

"It's not like that," I told him, though I wasn't sure what I meant by "it" and "that." Pepper was promiscuous, we all knew.

Pepper said, "You shouldn't have called him, Rainy. You're such a mother hen!" Then she took my phone, pausing only for a moment in her play. She said, "Honey, I'm hot on the slots is all. I'll be done in a minute, then life will return to normal. Stop it." She waited. Then: "Stop." She waited some more. Then: "I love you, bunny-bear." She waited. Then: "Yes, I do." She waited some more. Then: "I do, bunny-bear." Then she handed the phone back to me as if it were a bar of soap.

I felt like an idiot. Was I a meddlesome mother hen?

"You said *a minute*," said Nancy. "I heard you."

"I lied," said Pepper.

"Pepper," I said, "you go with Nancy to get your fiddle and I'll keep your seat warm."

Pepper paused to glance at me. "You'd do that?" Then she smiled her irresistible, just-love-me smile.

"Sure," I said. "I'll keep working it until you get back."

Levon said, "That's fair."

"I don't know that we can get back in time," said Nancy.

"Then I can't leave," Pepper said sadly.

Nancy stepped up close and said, "Fuck this up and I'll fire you."

It was an empty threat, Pepper knew. The nearest decent fiddler was in Elko and Nancy would have to pay him more than she wanted. And then it'd ruin her angle because we were booked as an "all-girl" band.

I stared at Pepper and she stared at Levon and he stared at Nancy and Nancy folded her arms as if to say, *Well?*

11

Maybe it occurred to Pepper that we'd all get fired. "Okay," she said at last, "let's go."

Nancy grabbed her by the hand, and they were gone.

I started in on the slot and soon had a good rhythm going. I was surprised that Levon stayed to watch me.

"What kind of chef?" I asked.

"Sauces." He was leaning against the machine on my left. I was getting prickly in anticipation of the spinning fruit. The guy who invented the slots was a genius for making the three wheels stop in sequence instead of all at once. Thwock: cherry! Thwock: cherry! Thwock: lemon!

"I didn't know there was a chef who did nothing but sauces," I said.

"Almost everything needs a sauce," he said.

I recalled the breaded eggplant I'd had the previous night at Te-Moak's "fine dining" room. I had wanted to treat myself. But the eggplant was swimming in a too-sweet brown sauce that made me wonder, *Who thought this syrupy mess would make the meal "fine"?*

Now I knew.

"Is that all you do?" I asked. "Sauces?"

He smiled at me. "I make a mean gumbo."

Kai, my boyfriend—who was earning his Ph.D. in library science—called himself a chef. A few months back, he had used a chunk of his student loan to buy a stainless-steel barbecue rig, which he chained to a tree behind our apartment building. His aspiration was to win a national BBQ contest. Pulled pork was his specialty. "He's a narcissist," my mother said. I was surprised she even knew the word.

"He's an academic," I said. "His head's in a different place."
"Yeah," my mother said. "Up his ass."

Levon was watching me intently, though I couldn't tell whether it was me or the machine that held his interest. Gambling has never been my thing. My brother, an actuary at an insurance company, recommended buying lotto tickets the way some people recommended getting flu shots and taking vitamins "just in case." I know, why would an actuary—who knows all about probability and statistics—bother with lotto?

Maybe there was something about America's wide-open spaces and go-for-broke optimism that made people like me and Mark believe that we could make our own luck. Every time I drove my old VW bus across Nevada for yet another gig, it felt like making bad bets was my addiction. Then I'd promise myself, *All right, this is it, time to stop*. But did I ever stop?

I fed the machine another nickel. The wheels spun. "This is my life," I joked. "Lots of expectation and no payoff."

"Too bad," Levon said.

Then the wheels clicked into place: one-two-three, a pot of gold! Before I knew what had happened, nickels were cascading out of the machine's chrome mouth. It was like a dream, that metallic stream spilling through my fingers. I was on my knees. I was making giddy girlish noises like a kid opening Christmas presents. Levon stood behind me to keep the crowd back. One of the tellers helped me rake the take into cardboard buckets. I was breathless and half dizzy.

After the cashier gave me seven one-hundred-dollar bills, four twenties, and a handful of change, Levon put his arm through mine and walked me to the parking lot. Outside, the sky was purple above the treeless mountains. I thought I smelled the nutty, roasted scent of burning leaves. I loved how things change so fast in autumn, especially in Nevada's high desert, where seasons were so much more pronounced than in Berkeley, the crowded college town I called home.

Levon took off his Stetson and turned as if to offer me a dance. He said, "Let's run away, right this minute."

He made it sound like the most reasonable suggestion.

Only then did I remember that the cash wasn't mine. And it wasn't much cash at all, certainly not enough to run away with. Then I wondered, *How much cash is enough to run away with?*

"Where would we go?" I asked.

He smiled. "Wherever we want."

"It's just seven-hundred dollars, Levon."

"It's more than you had yesterday," he said. "More than you'll have next week."

He was right. And I was surprised that it tempted me.

"That may be true," I said, enjoying the moment and playing it out. "But it's not mine, it's Pepper's."

"She's not the one with the magic hands," he said.

I looked down at my hands. Drummer's hands. There *were* magic in a way, weren't they?

"With hands like that," he continued, "you got nothing to be scared of."

"I'm not scared," I said. But then, as I thought about it,

I realized I was scared plenty because wasn't I was always just two paychecks away from broke? And wasn't my mother right? I was six months away from thirty. Good things should have happened by now. Really. What the fuck had I been doing with my time?

I sighed. "I've got to gig in half an hour."

"I make a mean gumbo, Rainy." He winked at me again.

"You've got a job too," I said.

"I could show you the mountains," he said. "You've never seen places like I could show you."

We were already at 4,295 feet in Winnemucca.

"You mean those?" I pointed to the purple silhouette in the distance.

"Canyons back there," he said, "and aspen and a waterfall you'd never imagine. There's lots more to it than it looks."

"Sounds nice, Levon."

"Come find out."

I laughed a nervous laugh to break the spell. "Why don't you come to the gig," I said. "I'll buy you a drink."

"Can't do that," he said. "I've got places to go."

"Mountains," I said. "Sure."

"And more," he said, serious now.

"Even without the jackpot?"

"Well, Rainy, I'm taking the jackpot."

Suddenly I understood why I was feeling so fluttery and dream-woozy. I was about to be robbed! Somehow I'd known this was going to happen.

"It's not my jackpot to give," I said.

"I'm gonna take it whether you give it or not," he said. He was standing casually, close enough that I could smell cigarette smoke on him and spicy cologne. He held his hat in one hand. His other hand, the hand I feared, was idle at his side.

Feeling weak and sick, I groaned inwardly. I wanted to retrieve the magic of the previous moments, but it was far gone now, like a lone swift circling high overhead.

"This isn't funny, Levon." I fought to steady my voice.

"Give over the cash," he said, "then you can go to your gig."

"Like that's all I care about?" I said. "Like I wouldn't go to the police?"

When he fitted his cowboy hat back on his head, I nearly flinched. He said, "You and me shared something. We're sharing something now."

When I didn't answer, he said, "I just want the money."

"What if I refuse?" I was crying now, hating myself for this.

"You won't refuse," he said.

"I might." Through a blur of tears, I glanced behind me. It was dark. Nobody was coming out of the casino.

When I turned back to Levon, he was smiling at me in a way that made me want to cry some more.

Levon held out one large hand.

Would the police call this a robbery?

I pictured myself laid up in my motel room with a black eye, watching reality shows on cable and crying for days.

Then, like the blast of a diesel horn, the double doors of the casino slammed open and five women walked out. The kind of women I had always mocked, with their cute kitten sweatshirts and black-rooted mullets. They stopped on the concrete skirt at the entrance and each lit a cigarette.

I waved to them: "Hey, ladies!"

They waved back. One called, "Hey, doll!"

Then I said to Levon: "I've got to go."

"I wish you wouldn't," he said.

I turned and walked away, clutching my messenger bag, tempted to run and nearly cringing with every step. It took me too long to get my keys into the door of my van. Once inside, I sobbed with relief. I saw in my rear view that Levon hadn't moved. He was watching me, though it was too dark to read his expression. I had a fleeting urge to run him over.

Five minutes later, when I pulled into Te-Moak's lot, I hadn't stopped trembling. I told myself I wasn't to blame for what had just happened. But I didn't want to tell anybody about it either, not even Kai.

You're not a victim, I told myself. *You don't need rescue.*

It made me sick to listen to pep-talking like that. I had always wanted to be tough. But what did that mean? Big girls don't cry?

It was dark already and surprisingly chilly, the moon like a distant streetlight. I phoned Kai.

He said: "Have you had enough?"

"You're so full of shit, Kai."

"That's why you love me," he said.

I knew he was right. "It's been a long day."

"Did Nancy act out?"

"It was Pepper this time," I said. "Do you miss me?"

"Every hour. If you were here right now, know what I'd do?"

"Ask me for twenty bucks, probably."

"After *that*," he said.

I closed my eyes and tried not to think of the long drive home. I said, "When are you going to get a job, Kai?"

"Is that why you called? Shouldn't you be on stage right now?"

From the nearby interstate ramp, I heard a truck whine as it shifted down, its driver probably eager for a casino stop.

I said, "Some guy asked me to run away with him tonight."

"I assume some guy is *always* asking you to run away with him. You're a drummer in an all-girl country band."

"I was tempted," I said. "For just a moment."

"I can't blame you for that," he said. "Your life is shit."

"You really mean that?"

"Which part?"

"My life is shit?"

"I'm trying to be sympathetic," he said. "Sounds like you need it."

I wiped at my eyes. I didn't want him to hear me crying. At last I said, "I just want it to be better than this."

Then I understood what I'd wanted from Levon Little: I wanted all of his lies to be true, about aspens and waterfalls way up in the canyon of those mountains—about the possibility of running away. Jesus, life is cruel.

Kai said, "I'd be there if I could."

I almost believed him. "I'm late."

"I hope you mean for your gig."

I liked that I could tell him anything and he'd make a joke of it. Sometimes I hated it, too.

Then he said, serious now, "I know you're the one holding things together out there."

"That's what drummers do," I said.

"You're good," he said. "You're solid."

I thought of making a joke of this. But then, like a sigh, I said, "Love you."

"That's all I need to know," he said. "Later, my little gator." Then he was gone.

On my way to the stage, I surprised myself by turning abruptly and striding towards the kitchen. The kitchen was down the same hall as the staff lounge. That's where we got our one free meal a day: a club sandwich with a handful of chips. The skinny security guard, slouched at the cordon that marked the employees' corridor, nodded to me as I breezed past. "Sup?" he said. When I got to the smelly maw of the kitchen and faced its two huge swinging doors, I stopped dead. If Levon was in there, concocting mediocre sauces for overpriced entrées, what would I say to him? I still had a pocketful of cash. I pushed through the doors and nearly ran into two servers carrying full trays as big around as wagon wheels. Two prep cooks were chopping vegetables at a long stainless-steel counter. Two others were tending pots at the huge stoves. The chef—a tall black man, wearing whites, with a pink rose pinned to his toque—peered into a big pot and said: "What the hell is *that* supposed to be?"

Did I see Levon standing at the steamy slop sink—loading a cart of dirty dishes into the washer, his head wrapped in a red kerchief?

No. It was a lanky Levon lookalike. Nevada was crowded with Levons, hungry caballero wannabes toiling for low pay and dreaming of a small break.

"You're in my kitchen."

I turned to the chef, who towered over me, his face as dark as dreamless sleep.

"Yeah," I said. "I'm looking for somebody."

He regarded me the way he might have regarded a tentative soufflé, like I looked near collapse. Then he said it again: "You're in my kitchen."

"Levon Little?" I said.

"Do I know you?" He had an accent I couldn't place. His left coat sleeve showed a single red stain the size of a penny. He was leaning forward as if to inspect me.

"I'm the drummer. In the band. Have you heard us? Country music?"

"Country," he said, as if to test the word.

"You know, Willie Nelson, Hank Williams, Loretta Lynn? Old school stuff."

"No," he said. "That's not *my* country."

I imagined some polyrhythmic Nigerian tune with pizzicato stringwork and a burbling kalimba counterpoint.

"You should check us out," I said. "It's live music."

"As opposed to dead music?" He had a scar at the corner of his left eye. Possibly made by the flick of a very sharp knife.

"I know you're busy," I said. "I'm just looking for Levon Little."

"Why should I care about Levon Little?"

"I didn't say you should care, I just asked if he worked here."

"You angry at me?" he said. "You come here to *harass* me?"

"I'm angry at Levon Little, this squirmy little fuck who wears a cowboy hat and a fat turquoise-studded belt—"

"No, you come in here and *say* you're looking for this, this cowboy but what are you really looking for?"

How was I supposed to answer that? I *was* looking for trouble. I was looking for answers. I was looking for restitution. And satisfaction. I know, I was asking for too much. Always.

The clatter of plates in my ears, my brow dripping with sweat, the soapy scent of dish detergent filling my nose, I stood there looking at this big chef who seemed to think I was a spy from the Health Department. I wasn't nearly as angry as I should have been, but I must have been scowling. I didn't know how to explain that it had nothing to do with the chef or his noisy, steamy kitchen. But I was too far gone to utter an explanation.

The only thing I knew for sure was that I was late for our first set. They'd start without me. That's just how it goes: you start no matter what—without drums or fiddle or whatever. Nancy would be singing "Blues Eyes Crying in the Rain" and flirting with the heavy drinkers up front because she wanted tips and that's what you do when you're in the spotlight: give people something to dream on.

BOOM, LIKE THAT!

Low tide, dark night. Lucky thing, it allows Jeton to walk the half mile across the reef to Kwajalein. The short cut. He's got to walk fast, watch for Security Patrol, and get across before the Security boat motors by with its sun-bright spot. He has to walk careful too, watch that he doesn't slip and cut himself on the coral, which is sharp like fish knives. Salt water will ruin the leather Nikes he borrowed from Cousin Mike. But fuck it.

He watches the lights of the 9:00-PM ferry on its way back to Ebeye. The last boatload of ri-Majeḷ returning for the night to their little lump of sand. And curfew begins now.

It takes a long time, this careful walking in dark water.

As he sloshes through tide pools, slipping every other step, cursing the reef, he almost wishes a rogue wave would reach over from oceanside and pull him into the depths—then Nora would be sorry, drowned Jeton washed up on Emon beach where Nora takes her morning swim.

They met at a soccer game when his high school played

the American high school. Ebeye boys run fast and play barefoot—they know this scares the American boys. They beat the Americans 5/2. Jeton plays goalie. He is good at diving for the balls. And he is unafraid of players rushing the goal. He has lost one tooth already from a crack-up at the net. "You could win a scholarship playing the way you do," Nora told him after the game. "You're damned reckless, you know that?" She was flirting, he knew right away. He offered her a cigarette and she said, "Are you crazy?"

"Yes," he said.

That's all it took. Boom, like that.

She loves him. She has said this many times. But she must fly home tomorrow. Four thousand two hundred miles east, back to the States. She will attend college while he finishes his last year of high school on Ebeye—if he can get back into high school. Nora does not know that he has lost his seat in class. He has been absent too much.

What is four thousand miles to Jeton? He has flown to Guam twice. One thousand three hundred miles. That was far enough. Nora says maybe he can go to college in the States. Win a scholarship. They could see each other, she says

Jeton knows she is lying, trying to make everything OK.

Nothing is OK anymore. This morning he called her on his cousin's cell phone. When she answered he said, "I'm gonna die if I don't see you, bellen."

He heard her sigh the kind of sigh he hears his younger sister make when she looks at the mail-order catalogue from the States, at all those things she knows she can't ever buy.

"I know, it's hard," Nora said.

He held that hot little bit of plastic phone to his ear and listened to the static. It sounded like rain splatter against wet sand.

"I own a fourth of that island," he said, desperate for justification.

"You mean your grandmother does," Nora corrected.

"Same thing, bellen."

Bellen: "partner," "mate," "wife" in his language.

"You know you can't come over now," she said, sounding weary—because he's been banned from Kwajalein. Everyone has heard about how Nora's parents caught him and Nora fucking on her patio.

When Jeton passes the boys on Ebeye, they cluck their tongues and grin. Some show him the thumbs-up. When he was younger—last year—this might have made Jeton proud. Now it just makes him shake his head sadly. He wishes he could tell the others how painful every thought of Nora is.

Jeton's grandmother gets a check every few months for her part of leasing Kwajalein to the Americans. It's been enough to buy her a condo on Guam, a new Nissan Altima LX every year, a pork farm in Manilla, but not enough to give to her huge family, every one of them with an empty hand held out. Still, she offered to buy Jeton a used Sentra and set him up in the taxi business on Majuro, the capital. Majuro island is one mile wide and 34 miles long and 300 miles from here. They've got a couple of discos and a copra plant and five different churches. Big deal. Jeton pictures himself driving the dusty roads of Majuro all day for fifty cents a ride, living in a room behind the Ambassador Hotel, drinking beer on the pier with the other boys until the sun sets, spending his nights looking to hook up with a pretty likatu.

Fuck that.

"They can't keep me from coming over," he told Nora.

"They'll put you in jail, is that what you want?"

He laughed. Ebeye's jail is a white-washed cinder block building the size of a boat house, surrounded by chain link fence.

"Jeton." Nobody has said his name like that, like it was a valuable secret. He imagined a lifetime of her saying his name, her lips inches from his ear. He could smell the strawberry shampoo of her hair, the flowery scent of her body lotion—she sunburns easily. He wanted to touch her. He imagined the two of them lying on the beach after curfew, the half-moon bright on her knowing face: she pulls down his shorts, nibbles at his belly to make him laugh, kisses him until he aches with impatience.

She gave him everything.

When they were loving each other in her narrow bed in the cold air-conditioned darkness of her room—after he had sneaked over while her parents were at work—they both made promises he believed they would never break.

She said, "You're the one, Jeton, you're the only one."

Other girls— ri-Majel girls—have said this to him. But ri-Majel girls say whatever comes into their heads. American girls are different. They believe in "going steady," they believe in having one man for life.

Jeton promised to make Nora happy always.

Now she says she has to leave. And he believes her. She says she will write to him once or twice a week. And he believes her, even though he has no computer for email. She says their time will come. And he wants to believe her. But he suspects that once she flies away, he will never see her again. He could tolerate this if only she could convince him that the separation sickens her the way it has sickened him.

Is he baka for having believed her? There is a term American boys use to describe this: *pussy whipped.*

"How was the party?" he asked her over the phone. Her going-away party.

"It wasn't the same without you," she said.

He knew she was telling him what he wanted to hear. He knew she had a good time, though she said she danced only with Britt, her girlfriend.

"I've got to see you," he insisted.

She said nothing and he knew that in her head—in her ettōṇak, her awake dreams—she was already on that plane, already back in the States, going to college, dating other boys and thinking of a "major" and a life Jeton can't begin to understand.

"I will write," she promised.

"Sure," he said. "Long letters."

When he handed the phone to his cousin, his cousin was looking at him like the time he got a big fish hook pulled through the palm of his hand. He said, "Jeton, you know, the phone—your voice—it goes up into space, hits a satellite, then bounces back, a hundred thousand miles, man, your voice is traveling just to get from here to there." He pointed across the reef to Kwajalein, which they could see from the dock: a flat stretch of green in the distance.

A hundred thousand miles.

Now: something stutters and skips past his feet. A shrimp scuttering to safety.

Americans like to come out here with flashlights to hunt for shells at low tide. Some aren't careful and the high tide catches them, sweeps them out and they are never found. All of this is a mystery to them, the water, the reef, the life the ri-Majel used to know. The ri-Majel used to be great navigators, great canoe builders. They knew how to read the waves and they made secret charts with sticks and cowries shells that enabled them to travel anywhere they pleased. No one knows how to do that anymore, except at the Allele Museum on Majuro, where two old men work year-round hacking out ceremonial tipñōls, sailing canoes, for tourists to see.

Jeton once took Nora to Pikeej in his uncle's speed boat. Pikeej is uninhabited, an overgrown coconut plantation with many hidden ruins from the World War Two, Japanese bunkers and huge oil tanks rusted orange. "Oh, God, Jeton, this is so cool," Nora said as they combed through the jungle. Jeton had a machete, wasps bobbed over their heads, the air was sweet with the scent of kōṇo blossoms. They found a grassy mound that could have been a grave site or a buried ammo dump. There they slipped off their clothes and looked at each other in the filtered light. Then they kissed and kissed until their lips were raw and there was nothing left to do but exhaust each other another way.

Why can't she see that life for them could be like this always?

Jeton comes ashore at last, wet up to the knees of his khakis. As he walks, his borrowed Nikes sound like soggy mops against a tile floor.

Nora lives in one of the new pre-fabs at this end of the island. They all look alike and, for a moment, Jeton panics, hidden in the shadow of someone's central air. He doesn't know if he can remember the right duplex.

If they catch him what can they do?

Last night, while drinking, one of the older men said to him: "Loving American likatu is no big deal. Everyone has a story of loving American girls."

This is what he fears, he realizes, that he is not special, that there is nothing in him that will make him different from anybody else. Doesn't matter if his grandmother owns one fourth of Kwajalein. Doesn't matter if he would've been a prince in another life. What is he now, right now? Maybe this is what Nora wonders.

Here comes the Security pickup with its big light. Lucky thing there are no dogs on Kwajalein, all that barking. Jeton scrambles farther into the shadows just as Security shoots its light where he was crouched. Truck slows to a stop, engine grumbling, light snaking through the dark stubbled yard between the pre-fabs, back porches, bamboo fence, gas grills, locked-up bicycles. Jeton pants, sucking air through his mouth, balled up behind a low fence. Shameful to be caught this way, like a shrimp curled under a rock.

Then the light is gone suddenly, the truck rumbling on.

Jeton stands up, pushes the hair from his eyes, smooths it back. He can smell his sweat below his English Leather cologne. Nora says she likes his smell. Ri-Majeḷ girls want you sweet like flowers.

He finds the right duplex—Nora's mother put up a family name plate over the door bell, their name burnt into a slab of wood. Jeton leaves his Nikes by the back door, smells the warm-fishy odor rising from them. The door is unlocked. Nora explained that this is why Americans love Kwajalein—it's like a small town, she said, you can leave your door unlocked at night. Jeton smiles at this.

It's so cold inside Nora's house Jeton shivers. Her cat, Simon, greets him, curling around his leg. A blue light gleams from the kitchen counter like a buoy in the distance. The house smells of chocolate cookies and ginger spice. Even in the dark it all looks familiar. He could live here, though he wouldn't clutter it up with all these little things, baskets and glass and books.

Carpet is thick as grass. Two minutes and Jeton is up the stairs. The door is closed to the room of Nora's parents. Nora says, old as they are, her Mom and Dad still have sex. This makes Jeton smirk. It is something he would never say about his own mother and father.

He hesitates outside Nora's room, fingers pressed hard against her closed door. He does not want to scare her.

Slowly he eases the door open. Simon squeaks its bird-like meow behind him. He closes the door in the cat's face. Then the room envelopes him in Nora's baby-powdery, girlish-sweet smell. Tears burn at the corners of his eyes. Nora! The posters of pretty-faced rock stars on the wall, the crowd of stuffed animal toys on the bureau, and on the neat desk top the conch shell that Jeton gave her for Christmas. She uses it as a paperweight.

Her narrow bed, neatly made.

Her big suitcase on wheels stands next to it.

Jeton sits, nearly falls, into her desk chair and stares at her empty bed.

Gone!

The difference between Kwajalein and Ebeye starts with the streets, Jeton decides. Here they are wide and paved and bright with electric light. The houses are neat, they all look alike, the yards are clear of motorbikes, scrap wood, trash, and chickens, and everything everywhere is green.

Jeton prefers Ebeye. Or Majuro. The haphazard houses and the sandy streets that curl and twist like vines and the animals that run freely and the children playing everywhere you turn and the cooking smells and the women singing and the laundry flagging from the lines over the dirt yards—all of this feels good. The Americans' place seems empty and haunted like Japanese ruins on Jaluit.

Here it is, Britney's house. Plastic Chinese lanterns of many colors glow from the bambooed patio. Jeton hears several girls talking, laughing. Sleepover.

Far from the patio fence, Jeton crouches at the trunk of a palm tree and listens. He can't make out what they are saying. Maybe talking about hot boys. Maybe talking about college. Who can tell with girls?

When there is a lull in the chatter, Jeton whistles. It is his special whistle, sounds like hissing and bird squeak at the same time. Everyone in his family does this whistle. Nora has teased him about it. "You think I'll answer *that*, like a dog or something?"

He whistles again. Now the girls whisper severely to one

another. A wasp's nest. Then he hears his name, like a curse on their lips. *Jeton, it's Jeton.*

And he knows that he has made a mistake. He should run, he should leave Nora alone, he should give her space, something Americans are always talking about. He is making trouble. But he can't go, he won't go. Not now. He will take his punishment, whatever it is, like the day he reefed his uncle's boat, like the time he insulted his grandfather by patting him on the head like a child, like the night he got drunk and rode his brother's bicycle off the pier.

The patio door opens, a paw of yellow light leaps into the yard, and Nora—unmistakable silhouette—walks towards him. The pink of a nearby street lamp lights her face. It is the face of a smart woman. Mālōtlōt. Wide, round freckled cheeks, a nub of a nose, big eyes like his own, dark lashes and dark brow. The kind of woman who could live happily on an outlying atoll. Who would not cringe from cleaning fish. Who would not complain when the rains came.

She is popular, she has said, because she is not pretty like those models in the Nordstrom catalog who scare Jeton because they look so mij. Dead. "Who could love them?" he asked her. "Why do Americans think these creatures are jouj?" Questions like these delight Nora: he can make her smile. This is how it should be always.

Tonight she wears a rock band t-shirt—"Metallica," it says— and white shorts and her white Birkenstocks. Tall, long legs, head up like she was walking at graduation. A woman who would sail with him through Toon Milu pass, north to Rongelap or Bikar or far-away Bokak.

What can he say to make her smile now?

He remains crouched, out of respect. He wants a cigarette, something to do with his hands.

"Jeton, what are you doing?"

His listens for love in her voice, a voice so much lower than any ri-Ṃajeḷ woman or girl he knows. Americans talk deep in the throat with flat words.

"I die when I don't see you, Nora."

"How did you get here?"

"Walked."

"Across the reef? Are you crazy?"

"Yes."

"Jeton." Sighing, she kneels near him. Her freckles he can see now: a thousand islands he wants to inhabit.

He says, "I don't want you to go." The words hurt like fish bone in his throat, make his eyes sting. As he wipes at them, he sees the other girls peering from behind the patio door.

"What would I do here?" Nora says. He hears gentle goodbye in her voice.

He shrugs. "We could have fun."

He wants more than fun. He knows she knows that.

She sighs. "We have been over this several times."

"You and me could do it, lijera, we could live on a island, just like we dreamed. You'd like it."

"I'm seventeen, Jeton, what do I know about living on an atoll?"

"You could learn. You and me could learn. You *love* it here, you said so."

"I'm *seventeen*!"

He says nothing, only stares at her in a way he knows she

finds charming. This is something she likes about him, how he will not argue, how he waits her out.

"Why does this make you smile?" she asks.

"Seventeen, Nora. You can do anything."

"And that's what I want to do—anything and everything. Things I can't do if I'm stuck on a tiny island out here in the middle of nowhere."

"Nowhere?" There is no equivalent for *nowhere* in his language. Ejjelok maybe: nothing.

"I didn't mean it like that," she says quickly.

He sees regret in her face, that sorry look he has seen after his mother loses a day's wages at cousin Amsa's weekly cock fight. *Gone*, her look says, *it's gone*.

Jeton weighs the American words of loss: *nothing, none, not, no*.

His lijera lays her hand lightly over his, brings him back abruptly, but he can hardly see her for the tide rising in his eyes.

She says, "Jeton, don't you have any plans?"

"College, Nora? I'm no good at school."

"You could win a scholarship to college, the way you play soccer. Maybe start with junior college."

"In the States? You don't want your ri-Majel boy in the States with you."

"I didn't say we'd be together, Jeton. I'm talking about your future, not about us."

"You are my future."

"I am your girlfriend, that's all. And tomorrow I'm going fly away. That's a fact you have to accept."

"I don't want you to forget me," he says.

"Why would I forget you? How could I?" She lowers her head to meet his eyes.

Sitting in the half dark, palm tops clattering above them in the breeze, the girls spying on them from the patio, Security Patrol prowling somewhere nearby—Jeton understands that he wants more from Nora than she can give him. If only he could describe his feelings, he might change her mind. But there are not enough words and they are not the right kind of words.

"You will have other boyfriends," he says.

"And you won't ever have another girl friend? You want to mummify me or something? I've got my life, you've got yours. Maybe you'll find your way to the States and we'll see each other. Maybe I'll decide I'd rather be here and I'll come back. Who can say? Anything can happen, just like you and I happened. You can't hide from that, you can't stop that."

He wishes she could take his hand, kiss it the way she used to, lay her face against his neck. . . .

"You are right," he says. "I am just a boy, I don't know what I'm doing."

She smiles at him. This is what he wants, that softening, that kindness. But he is lying to her. He believes that she is making a terrible mistake, that she will be in her big, cluttered American house years from now and she will look out at her big empty yard with its green green grass and she will think of the life she could have had here with Jeton. But he knows that he cannot stop her. He knows that, as with certain lovely fish, he has to stay clear or risk great harm.

She says, almost in a whisper, "I'm not sorry for what we had, are you?"

"No, I am not sorry," he says. She will haunt him, he knows. He will see her always in his head: Nora running, Nora laughing, Nora waving to a friend, Nora's long fingers combing through his hair, Nora kissing him on the nose.

"Are you going to be all right?" she asks.

"I'm cool." Saying what the American boys always say.

"You're not going to do something crazy?"

"I will hang out till day, then take the ferry back, OK?"

"Why don't you sleep on Brit's patio—we'll go inside." She offers him her kindest smile. "Please."

It is impolite to deny an offer of hospitality. And he wants to make her happy. And he would like to be near her. Maybe in the morning she will change her mind. He knows this is a slim chance but it is more than he had a few minutes ago.

She does not kiss him when she says goodnight from the back door of Brit's house. He is sitting on the patio hammock, which swings slightly beneath him. The patio smells like candy sweetness. Girls. Jeton nods his goodnight to Nora, watches her close the door and disappear into the darkness beyond the kitchen. She feels sorry for him. That is not good. She will return in the morning to find him curled on the hammock like a stray dog. And he will smell of tonight's hard walking. And she will be eager to get home because she is excited about her trip, her plane flying off tomorrow afternoon. She's going places. 4,250 miles. And he is going to Ebeye. He is not going to college. He is not going to the States.

He does not lie down; there is no sleep in him. He leaves the patio, the girlish sweetness still in his lungs. Sadness makes his heart feel like it is a piece of water-soaked wood. Sodden and sluggish. He stands in the street and stares up at the duplex, at the light in Brit's window. He imagines the girls will whisper all night long. They will give Nora advice, tell her how to dump Jeton in the morning.

He doesn't know how long he stands out here. A long time.

Then he hears a truck approaching. Security Patrol. But Jeton does not think fast enough to run. And suddenly it looks like morning, so much light around him.

He turns to the light. Truck light.

"Don't move, son."

It is the big-bellied black American officer named Ulysses. With a grunt of effort he steps out of the pickup. He reminds Jeton of his third uncle on his father's side. Except this man has no sideburns. The officer squints through the smoke of his cigarette which he keeps at his mouth. He has his right hand on the gun at his wide leather belt. His other hand holds a big flashlight. Truck's spot makes Jeton squint hard.

"You got I.D.?" the officer asks. He stands to one side of the truck. Garble stutters through the little black radio attached to his shirt pocket. Looks like the weight of him should pull him over.

Jeton slides his Velcro wallet out of his back pocket. Slowly. Everybody knows you have to move slow in front of Security.

The officer takes the wallet, flips it to the I.D. "Jeton DeGroen," he says. Flashlight on the I.D. "I heard about you. Your grandma owns half the island."

"A fourth."

The officer smiles, shakes his head like he knows something Jeton doesn't. "She gets a lot of money for that land. And I bet you see some of it."

Jeton wants to tell him that the land means nothing, it's always been here, it will stay here until the ocean decides to swallow it. He remembers what the teachers told him about how these atolls began. Coral attached itself to volcanoes and kept growing as the volcanoes sank. After a long time the volcanoes were gone, buried deep under water. But the coral remained, a circle of coral where the volcano used to be. That's what he feels inside him now, Nora gone but a deep crust left behind.

He says, "Grandmother wants to buy me a used Toyota so I can have a taxi business on Majuro."

"There you go."

"Taxi's not my style."

"Neither is obeying the law apparently." The officer flicks away his cigarette, turns his head to the radio at his shoulder and says, "Got a code 40. Bringing him in, ten-four." Then he says to Jeton: "What's your excuse for breaking curfew, little man?"

"I don't need excuse."

"You better think one up."

In another life he would've been a prince.

When Jeton doesn't answer, the officer says, "Man, in the States we'd send you to a work farm." He lights another cigarette with a silver Zippo lighter, like all the Security have, doesn't seem in a hurry to go. Maybe because Jeton is so relaxed. Late night like this makes some people want to stand around and talk. Always somebody talking late on Ebeye—Jeton hears them every night, two or three people off here and there, smoking and talking.

"Got a smoke?" Jeton asks.

"Take the pack, little man." The officer tosses the cigarettes to him.

Like a fish flying from a wave, Jeton leaps forward—not for the cigarette pack but for the officer's big waist. Tackle him, he tells himself. Tackle him, then run away. It's not a plan exactly, it just happens. Boom. It reminds him of soccer, of diving for a shot that saves the game, his reflexes so quick, his jump so surprising, that it makes the American girls on the sidelines cheer, even though they aren't supposed to cheer for the ri-Majel, and then one of them, he notices, the tall, pretty one, flashes him her smile and Jeton knows he shouldn't give a second look, he knows that American girls are trouble, everyone says so, he really should leave them alone. Do not smile back! he cautions himself. But she is tall and freckled and beautiful, Miss America, and he is the center of her attention now—he remembers this so clearly, the cheering in his ears as loud as waves crashing over him. Of course he smiles back. Boom, like that.

JACKPOT

I owe a lot to Tiny Britten. She hired me to drive her all over the desert to search for mustangs. She wanted one dead or alive. Live ones are better, but she didn't know the first thing about keeping animals. Neither did I. "You're my cowboy," she'd say, lifting one of my hands off the steering wheel. I've got big hands. "Grip's important," Tiny said the first time we met. She stood there hanging onto my handshake like she was about to arm wrestle and yank me over. So I pulled a little my way and she smiled. I smiled back. Then her husband, Mars, said, "Let me see," and Tiny Britten handed me over, so I gripped his hand too. All of us had big hands. "You must work hard," he said.

The truth is, I'd been working hard on the slots for a few months. I had the fever bad. It was just after I'd been fired for dealing lousy in Reno, because I couldn't remember all the cards. Dealing twenty-one from two decks all night wore me out. So I played blind, not counting cards, and I lost lots of the casino's money. It's always *their* money no matter whose pocket it comes from. I almost swung work at other houses until I got blackballed for dicking with one of the coin-toss machines at Harrah's. I was shoving it, trying to topple silver into the twenty-dollar hole. The security guards took me to a back office, and I thought they were going to punch me some, but they only snapped my photo and sent it all over town. They could have arrested me, but I wasn't worth it, they said. So I went east across the state, playing little casinos. I wasn't in the mood for work, and I figured if I found trouble, I'd head to Vegas, where the casinos wouldn't ride me, they've got so many big-timers to worry about.

I wasn't eating right, and I started drinking some, mostly screwdrivers because they're hard to ruin. Before I knew it, I was crazy for the slots. It was looking at all those coins—especially dollars and halves—that got me, those machines swollen with silver. And I was winning. It's the worst bet in the casino, even the amateurs will tell you. But when you're winning at slots, there's nothing like it because it's a real private thing. Just you and the machine, you can play as fast or as slow as you please. I'd work as many as four machines at a time all night until my hands were black from the coins and my fingers nearly numb and my shoulders hot with pain. But you can keep a streak only for a short spell. I slipped till I was playing nothing but nickels. By the time I saw Tiny Britten's ad in the Elko *Craigslist*, I was down to one cardboard bucket of them—about $36—and I knew I had to get away for a while to cool off and dry out.

Tiny asked no questions, and I suspected I was the only one who'd answered her ad. She wasn't offering any money, just room and board and some shares in her horse ranch, which wasn't built yet. All she had was a trailer on cinderblocks about fifty miles south of Winnemucca. We passed through Grass Valley, over the last range, took a turn onto a dirt road that wasn't more than a cow path, then I was lost. There was a black rocky range to one side and another far off to the other side that had a white streak across the middle, which Tiny said was salt.

Nevada can be pretty. But not here. We were in the stone-hard heart of the state. It's high desert—not your white-sand-and-big-cacti cliché but packed dirt studded with sagebrush as far as you can see, each bush the size of a basketball. From a distance they make the land look leprous. The mountains are nothing more than naked rock, so barren they made me wonder if hell could look worse. Nobody wanted this land. That's why it was wide open. Elsewhere—farther east—you'd find spring-fed meadows, fields of wheat, cattle grazing among pinion pine and juniper, mountains forested with bull pine. But not here.

I'd met Tiny in front of Aces High in Winnemucca, after waiting around until the top of my head was itchy from sunburn. "Looks like you've got smarts," Tiny told me. "Doesn't he, Mars?" "It's the glasses," he said. "They magnify his eyes." I was still wearing my casino outfit—white shirt and black pants with black shoes, what all casino workers wear, except mine hadn't been washed in weeks.

When we got to the "ranch," as Tiny called it, she gave me a cowboy hat and some new blue jeans that were too tight and cowboy boots that were too big. And I began that day, driving straight across the desert, doing all kinds of damage to the plant life. Tiny was always wearing her sunglasses, well pressed jeans, a long-sleeved cowboy shirt with snap pearl buttons and the light-colored cowboy hat (seven gallons, she said). She was tall and slump-shouldered and seemed to have spent most of her life indoors. She was that pale. She had shadows under her eyes from lack of sleep and, it's true, she slept little, maybe a few hours at a time. She spent most of her nights sitting in a lawn chair out back behind the trailer with a rifle and a bag of potato chips and a flashlight as big as a club. The first few nights, I didn't know what she was up to, so I went out finally and asked her, long after Mars had gone to bed. "What are you doing, Tiny?" She grinned at me. "Waiting for the expected," she said.

"Isn't driving like this illegal?" I asked her at the start. The truck was vintage, with four on the floor. It rattled over ruts and swayed, the shocks squeaking, as I steered up one slope and down another. The air was always chalky with dust.

Tiny kept looking from side to side like she was afraid of missing something. Or like maybe we were being followed by state troopers or poachers or I don't know what. She said, "Great thing about Nevada is mostly you don't have to worry about legal or illegal." Then she held out one hand like she was offering me everything I could see. "Look," she said. "It's wide open!"

The truth is, driving like that across the desert is illegal. There were signs, just off the main road that said so. I'd seen something on the news years ago that said chasing wild horses is illegal too. But these weren't the first illegal things I'd done.

There wasn't much to it except boredom. The desert stretched on and on, hill after hill, and Tiny Britten usually said nothing, her rifle aimed out the window. I would have asked her to drive some, only she couldn't. She had trouble coordinating the gas and the clutch, and she never watched where she was going, so she'd veer off, driving the truck into a ditch or racing headlong into a butte. It was queer behavior for a mechanical genius. An engineer, she called himself. Just the year before, she'd been helping an oil company look for deposits near Tonopah. That was the first she'd seen Nevada because, until then, she'd spent most of her life in school. She had a lot of ideas for inventions—the trailer was crowded with her drawings—but she didn't do anything with them. Besides some pressure-sensitive liquid sensor she'd made for an oil company, the only other Tiny Britten invention that ever got completed, as far as I know, was 50 gallons of Even-Steven, an alcoholic drink distilled from pine nuts and non-fat dry milk.

Drinking Even-Stevens was how Tiny and Mars spent most of their time together. They'd drink until they got real quiet and sleepy, and then they'd lie next to each other in a lawn chair and lick each other's hands. That's all they did, this *licking*. It made me prickly to watch them, so I tried to stay out of the way. But that wasn't easy, since the trailer was small. I wasn't about to go walking around, on account of rattlers. Outside there was nowhere to go anyway and nothing to look at except the ridge in the distance. And no shade except next to the silver propane tank at the side of the trailer. So I'd sit on the front steps, fanning myself with the hat Tiny had given me.

Sometimes Mars's retarded collie, Frank, joined me, though I wasn't too fond of his company. He'd lick my hand every time I reached down to pet him. And I'd get prickly again, thinking of Mars and Tiny. That's when I'd ask myself why I was staying on. But I had to admit that despite the inconveniences—or because of them—I was losing the urge to gamble.

Mars didn't join me and Tiny on the hunt until Frank disappeared. Mars claimed the poachers had gotten Frank. "What poachers?" I asked. He and Tiny smiled at me like I was stupid. Tiny said, "You've heard of poachers, Lawrence. They're people—" "Marauders," Mars corrected. "Exactly," said Tiny, "they're marauders who are always looking for a steal." Mars shaded his eyes with one hand and scouted the distance. "They got Frank for sure," he said. Tiny nodded in agreement. "Good old Frank."

I couldn't imagine why anybody would want Frank. But I didn't say so, because Mars was sensitive and kind of nervous, always halfway between laughing and crying. You never knew how he'd take an opinion. He was a former body builder gone flabby. Tiny said steroids had gotten the better of him.

Frank was an overweight collie with a too-narrow face and crossed eyes, his coat dusty and knotted and smelling like piss. He always gagged whenever he ate because he ate too fast, like he was afraid someone was about to take his bowl away. And he couldn't bark. "Talk to me," Mars would say. "Tell me what's on your mind, Frank." The dog would look up at Mars like he was about to whimper, his tongue dangling, his whiskers twitching. Then he'd heave with effort, but all you'd hear would be a grunt. Mars had had Frank for fifteen years and that was all he could make the dog do, but Mars didn't seem to mind. "He's like a brother," he said. Frank was always lying under the lawn chair while Mars sunbathed.

Sunbathing was what Mars did most of the time. He had great tan, wearing bikini briefs to show it off. But I don't think Tiny cared one way or the other. He and Tiny had met in Tonopah at the Money Bucket, where Mars was a barback. He was in his forties and she wasn't out of her twenties. Mars had been married once before to a woman who owned a gypsum mine. He lost her when she fell down an unfenced shaft hole. They're all over the desert—mine shafts about five feet square that drop straight down hundreds of feet. Because of all the brush, you won't see one until you're right at the edge. Mars was still in mourning when he met Tiny. He said, "Tiny was different, you could tell right off. Sensitive. Look at those little gray eyes." I did and Tiny grinned at me. He said, "She told me about the wild horses she'd seen while scouting for oil, and that was that—we figured wild-horse ranching was for us, because we could be our own bosses and get the animals for free." Tiny said, "Acreage out here goes for next to nothing." They had used Mars's insurance money to buy the trailer (used) and lots of supplies, like canned hams and blocks of cheese food. "It's been like a vacation," Mars said, "except for dealing with the chemical toilet."

When Mars joined us on the hunt, he lay in a lawn chair that Tiny had bolted to the flatbed. I would've gotten sick sprawled in the sun like that and jounced around all day long. But Mars didn't seem to mind. He said he wanted to find Frank, no matter what. When Tiny decided to make an overnight trip, she got real excited about it. She took charge of loading the truck, while I ran errands. All I could think about was having to sleep with rattlers around and tarantulas crawling out of holes at night to creep like hairy hands across my face.

We started out the same old way, heading south, early in the morning. It was still cool. Birds were noisy with singing. The clouds were sparse and high, the air sweet with sage. As the day went on, the sun burned through and all I could smell was truck exhaust.

We'd been driving for an hour or so when Tiny yelled, "Stop! Stop!" I stamped on the brakes. Billows of dust overtook us and it was minutes before I could see what she was excited about. "That's a hoofprint," she said, hopping out of the truck. I saw one print preserved in the hardened mud. "A pretty sight," Mars said, placing his big brown hand over it. "It gives me chills—" He stopped abruptly, half-crying. Then he laughed. "This is so exciting!" he said. Tiny wanted to dig it up as a souvenir. She got out a pick-ax and took a swing but missed, shattering the print. "I don't know much about the desert," I said, "but seems to me that print could've been there for years." Tiny was looking down at Mars as he picked up the pieces of the print like they were a broken plate. "Where there's one, there's hundreds," she said. "It's a matter of probability." That made me think of gambling and I started wondering if I'd taken a bigger risk than I'd realized coming out here with these two.

By the time we stopped for lunch, Tiny was in the mood to shoot something. She said she didn't feel right if she didn't fire the rifle at least once a day. I watched Mars spread a picnic blanket in the shade of a sandstone cliff, while Tiny aimed her rifle at objects on the horizon, where everything was watery with ripples of heat. "Blam blam blam!" she said. Mars said, "Here, take this," handing me a cheese sandwich, then one to Tiny, but she wouldn't take it. Maybe it bothered her to see us eating cheap, because the money was getting low.

Tiny decided she'd shoot one of the swallows that were darting to and from their nests in the shade of the cliff. "They probably taste like squab," she said, aiming. I told her there wasn't enough meat on those little birds to feed a cat. She shrugged. "Anything's better than cheese." For a while I watched the rifle barrel stir the air as Tiny followed the birds. Then I sat in the truck cab and looked at the map, though there was nothing to look at—no roads, no settlements, nothing but dry, dusty open country so hot the air seemed to buzz with meanness.

The report of Tiny's rifle sounded like the pop of a paper bag. The recoil kicked her onto the blanket, where she rolled over a bag of potato chips Mars was eating. "Look what you've gone," he said, pushing her off the crushed chips. She got up and looked around for her kill, but the swallows were done. "Here," Mars told her, "put some chips on your sandwich."

Tiny had brought several one-gallon thermoses of Even-Stevens, tossing each drink down in a small paper cup. I didn't drink any. The stuff tasted like bourbon mixed with buttermilk. Tiny and Mars drank cup after cup. "I miss Frank," Mars said, his chin quivering.

"Good old Frank," said Tiny. She poured herself another Even-Steven.

The sun was almost directly overhead, stealing shade from the cliff. Mars stretched out on the lawn chair in the back of the truck. I told him too much sun would ruin his skin.

"Do me a favor," he said. "Get me a drink." He wore little white cups over his eyes. A small pool of oil and sweat glistened in his navel. Either he had no body hair or he meticulously shaved himself.

"I'm going to send out the drone," Tiny announced, suddenly standing and emptying her paper cup. "It'll save a hell of a lot of gas."

"Does that mean we don't have much left?" I asked. We had two cans tied to the truck, but I hadn't checked what we had at the trailer.

"The drone will give us the big picture. We'll watch it over cocktails and crackers."

"You know how to live, Tiny." Mars smiled, his eyes still cupped. His skin was gleaming.

I said, "We really ought to have the truck repaired." The clutch was chattering and the valves clacking like rocks in a can. "Did you bring the tool box?"

Tiny shrugged and took another drink.

"It's dangerous being out here without tools," I said.

"We'll improvise," she said. "Like pioneers."

While Mars and Tiny finished a thermos of Even-Stevens, I counted the sagebrush as far as I could see, pretending they were horses. Then I made bets with myself about how my count would change when I tried again. The numbers were never the same.

A few hours later, we stopped in a dry creekbed, a good place to camp, said Tiny. She scanned the horizon with her rifle scope, then the binoculars. "Nothing moving but the heat," she said finally. The truck ticked as if about to explode. I pissed on the hood, expecting it to sizzle, but it only steamed. Mars was sleeping, sprawled—slack-jawed—on his chair.

"Is he all right?' I asked. "He looks oversunned."

"He loves it," said Tiny. She poured herself another Even-Steven, then sat in the shade of the truck.

I strung up the tarp and told Tiny to wake Mars so he could get some shade. She shook him. The sun cups fell from his eyes and he lolled his head back and forth, like he was drunk. "Ease up," he muttered. Tiny patted his cheek. She said, "Come over here and lie down, Mars." With her help, he stumbled off the truck, then sat there like an old Indian, his boobs limp and withered. Tiny offered him an Even-Steven, but he didn't seem to see it. "Dots," he said. "Goddamn dots all over the place."

"Too much sun," I said.

Tiny wanted to scout around before sunset, so we left Mars and hiked up a steep mound nearby. The drone had come back with footage of something dead in the distance. All was quiet except for the scratch of lizards scrambling over rocks. The sun was low, long shadows streaming from brush and boulders. A quarter mile away, a vulture hunkered over a dead animal. Tiny took a couple shots at it but missed. The bird lifted off with slow steady wingbeats. Tiny wanted to examine the dead animal, so we worked our way down, careful not to step where rattlers hide. What we found was a dog or what might have been a dog. Ants and vultures had done their work on it, little left but bones and bits of hair. It could have been a collie, but I didn't think it had Frank's colors. Tiny knelt like a hunter reading clues. "No signs of foul play," she said, poking the remains with her rifle barrel. "It could've been a coyote," I said. Tiny stood up and squinted at the sun. "I wouldn't mind bagging a coyote."

"They're just little dogs," I said. "You wouldn't want to shoot a little dog, Tiny."

"I'd shoot Lassie if I had to, Lawrence. This is about survival."

"We have provisions."

"Cheese?"

"And bread and potato chips."

"What we need is meat. Pork chops and T-bones. Or maybe rattlesnake."

"I like cheese just fine, Tiny."

"Rattlers taste like chicken, you know."

"I can live on cheese, thanks."

Tiny said, "You're not talking like a cowboy, Lawrence." She started flipping over flat rocks with her rifle barrel. "Let's shoot a couple of rattlers and cook them on a spit like shish kebab."

"I don't want shish kebab," I said.

She kicked over a slab of rock the size of a place mat. "Here's one." She crouched for a better view. "Sleeping soundly. Coiled like a piece of garden hose." It was a rattler three feet long and as fat as a toothpaste tube.

I said, "Leave it alone, Tiny."

She said, "Watch this guy's expression when I wake him."

"Don't," I said.

Tiny prodded the snake with the barrel. The snake jerked its head back and was flicking its tongue, its rattles rattling. Tiny pulled the rifle trigger but nothing happened. She pulled again. "Wait a minute," she said, like she was asking someone to stop talking. She'd forgotten to reload. The snake hissed. Tiny said, "Just a minute." The rattler hit her boot. Tiny jumped back and the snake hit her boot again. I was so light-headed from fear, I fell back into a clump of thistle. I saw Tiny swing her rifle like a bat. Then she reloaded and shot the snake twice, sand and snake bits flying in all directions. "I think that did it," she said. After she had her breath back, she tied the two biggest snake pieces to her belt, where they dangled, oozing blood.

It was dark when we got back to camp. Mars was gone. I lit a lantern while Tiny poured herself another Even-Steven. "Probably out for a walk," she said.

"The desert's no place for a walk at night," I said.

"Probably taking a leak," she said.

I called out for him. He didn't answer. Tiny started cleaning the snake, chopping and flailing with her bowie knife until her hands were covered with scales and guts. She was pounding the thing with the knife handle.

I sat on the tailgate of the pickup and watched the sky. It was a clear moonless night. I could smell the smell of suntan lotion from Mars's vacant lawn chair. After she was done with the snake, Tiny decided we should go looking for him. We called and called, but he didn't answer. Tiny swept the beam of her flashlight all around. To our surprise, Mars had been standing nearby the whole time, naked and silent, with a funny smile on his face.

"Hi, Mars. You see what we got?" Tiny held up half the battered rattler.

"He's not looking too well," I said.

"How do you feel, Mars?" Tiny took off her hat like she was about to introduce herself.

"Could be sun poisoning," I said. "Or dehydration."

"You hungry?" Tiny asked him.

"He's out of sorts, Tiny."

"This is not like him," she said. "He's probably sick."

"Maybe we should get him to relax," I said.

"You want to relax, Mars?" Tiny started walking to him and he started backing away. "Mars? It's me—Tiny?" Then she went for him and he took off, running. Tiny and I followed in the pickup, Tiny bringing along the rifle because, she said, "You never know what's out there."

I'd never seen anyone run like Mars. He was hurdling shrubs and rocks like a deer. We lost him finally because the truck couldn't make speed over the rough terrain. I scanned a circle with the headlights, but Mars was gone, so we stopped to listen. Tiny opened another thermos of Even-Stevens and this time drank straight from it.

"I should've winged him," she said, "just to slow him down."

"*Shoot* him?" I said.

"Just a nick." She pinched together a thumb and forefinger. "This much maybe."

"You don't want to shoot your husband," I said.

She took another drink. "I never knew he could run like that," she said. She drank some more, then peered through the dusty windshield. "He's out there, creeping around," she said. "Turn on the lights."

I switched on the headlights and there, not twenty feet from the truck, was a mule—a black, gaunt, weather-beaten animal probably half-stupid with hunger. It seemed startled to see us.

Tiny yelped: "A wild horse!" She propped the rifle on the dash as if to shoot through the windshield. "You ever see ears so big?"

The mule snorted, showing its dark teeth.

I said, "It's a mule, Tiny."

Tiny said, "Where's your lasso, Lawrence?"

I got a rope from the back of the truck. I'd never thrown a lasso in my life, but I promised Tiny I'd give it a try if the mule would stand still for it. I tried and tried and missed each try, while Tiny groaned and squirmed. "Come on, cowboy," she kept saying. The mule stood there staring like it had never seen people before. Maybe it hadn't. I got the rope around its neck finally. "Hold him!" Tiny shouted, jumping in her excitement. "Don't let go!" Behind me, she tied the rope-end around her waist. "We've got him now!" She yanked the rope and nearly threw me off-balance. The tug made the mule frantic. It bucked until the rope was cutting my hands. Tiny kept screaming, "Hold him tight, cowboy!" I wanted to tell her to shut up, but I was hurting too bad. When I glanced back, I could see I had all my problems tied to the end of that rope. So I let go.

Tiny said, "Hey!" and that was the last I saw of her. The mule dragged her off. A while later, somewhere in the distance, I heard a "Whoa!" but soon it was quiet except for a breeze stirring the sage. I waited around for the longest time, but nobody came back. So I ate two cheese sandwiches, then fell asleep on Mars's chair, the whole thing smelling like flowers because of him.

In the morning, I went back to the trailer, which I had some trouble finding. Frank was there, trotting around like he'd been out only for a walk. He's as ugly a dog as ever and he still gags when he eats, but he's not bad company. He sits under the lawn chair while I take the sun every day. Sometimes I share a thermos of Even-Stevens with him. Then I get up to take potshots at lizards and Frank trots out ahead of me to raise his nose at noises I can't hear. That's about all we do nowadays. Can't go anywhere because the truck's broken. We've got enough supplies to last for a while, so I'm looking at this as a vacation, a kind of jackpot I never thought I'd hit.

"Look at that," I say to Frank, waving a hand like I'm offering him the world. The old dog blinks at me and grunts.

SIX BLIND CATS

By the time Sonia realized the six kittens were blind, their mother was dead, crushed by a 40-foot RV speeding past her house. She found the kittens inside an old truck tire at the back of her garage. They hissed at her hand as she drew near.

She gathered them up—two handfuls—and nestled them into an antique hatbox filled with shredded newspaper. Using a turkey baster, she fed them goat's milk several times a day. She had been getting the goat's milk regularly from a neighboring farm because she was lactose intolerant. Sonia had no farm herself but she had two acres and some outbuildings.

As soon as the cats could wander, which was sooner than she had imagined, she realized she could not keep up with them. Herding six blind kittens all day? She had a full-time job, selling appliances at a big box store.

Her husband—a former merchant Marine who had jumped ship in Yokohama, Japan, twenty years previous—

was now married to a Japanese woman who, apparently, didn't mind that he had another wife.

Their son, now 32, lived in transitional housing in a city close to Sonia's. He'd been in and out of "homes" for nearly two decades. When he stayed on his medication, he could visit her. When he didn't stay on is medication, which was most the time, he got agitated and felt the need to wander. He had wandered into many people's homes. It was a miracle that he hadn't been shot. Sonia visited him every Saturday morning. If he was calm, they would play hearts or twenty questions until it was time for his lunch. If he wasn't calm, she would hold his hand while he rocked to and fro in his favorite chair and said, "Got to go, mom—got to go!"

In desperation, Sonia put the kittens in with her chickens. Her chickens were Dominiques, a heritage breed that had once been *the* American chicken but had gone out of favor after the rise of corporate farming. The chickens eyed the kittens warily. The kittens seemed fine with the arrangement, bumbling through the chicken house shavings and sunning themselves sleepily in the pecked-over chicken yard.

By the time they were grown, the cats had learned to shadow the chickens, nosing at their scaly heels and sniffing through their leavings. Sonia fed both at once, and often the chickens competed with the cats for the kibble.

She had never wanted cats. She wasn't a cat person. But, then, it seemed these weren't cats exactly. Also: Matt, her son, loved them. Apparently, their vulnerability made them especially appealing. Matt insisted that he become their caretaker, even though there wasn't much to do. Every Saturday he'd spend hours standing among the cats and chickens, watching them—admiring them.

When word got around about the cats, visitors came. Children clung to the wire fence and leaned forward to behold the blind cats. The cats scratched in the dirt like chickens, nodding their heads as they sniffed and foraged. Sonia called them Chicken Cats and sold the visitors her eggs, which many of the visiting children believed were cat eggs.

Matt helped sell the eggs. Nobody was more enthusiastic. His dedication and the change that had overtaken him made Sonia quietly, cautiously grateful.

Thanks to the increasing number of visitors, she was selling all of her eggs—and early. It occurred to her that she could get more chickens, sell more eggs, maybe branch out and sell souvenirs too. But then she reconsidered: 1) an old flock of chickens will not accept new members easily. The ensuing strife might ruin the remarkable harmony her current chicken-cats enjoyed; and 2) she would never again find—and she certainly couldn't create—another brood of blind cats. No, the small spectacle in her backyard was a one-time phenomenon and it would live only as long as the cats themselves. When they were gone, the visitors would disappear, and her life would return to normal.

By the time she came to this understanding, however, she had already ordered 500 bars of castile soap to sell as souvenirs. On the face of each bar, there was an etched figure of a blind cat. Yes, a cat wearing sunglasses and standing on its hind legs, a walking cane in one paw. Sonia had thought this would be cute but now she saw that it was, well, embarrassing. She didn't like cats all that much, not even her own.

With her son's help, she spent many nights wrapping each soap bar in clear cellophane. Matt was good at this tedious work (a red ribbon secured the clutch of wrap at one end of each bar). Still, Sonia felt foolish and callow shilling soap. She made a 10-cent profit on her first bar.

After her 50th sale, however, she realized that people *liked* the soap and that she could sell more, faster, if she put some effort into it. Now, when visitors leaned into the wire fence to stare at her chicken-cats, Matt walked behind them, calling, "Blind Cat soap. We have a limited supply!"

She sold 100 bars that weekend; 250 the next weekend; 275 the next.

Sonia was no dreamer. She had suffered enough disappointment and heartache to know that such good fortune could not last. Sure enough, the cats died surprisingly young, from an avian flu that also killed most of her chickens. Matt was inconsolable. When she visited him and held his hands and explained that it couldn't be helped, he wouldn't answer. He seemed to blame her. Soon after, he had a relapse and was once again heavily medicated.

What won't a mother do for her son? This question haunted her for weeks. She scoured animal rescue centers within a 100-mile radius, asking for blind kittens. She located a few blind cats but they were old. She put off buying more chickens. She had 1200 bars of Blind Cat soap in her garage.

Then she found two kittens that had been blinded by a bleach spill. When she went to pick them up, just twenty miles away, the rescue volunteer—a young woman who wore denim, her red hair tied in pigtails—said, "I *know* you—aren't you the woman with the blind cat farm?"

"It's not a farm," Sonia said. "But, yes, I had blind cats."

"It was, like, a tourist attraction?"

"No," she said. "I had visitors, people curious about how I had raised these cats—with chickens."

The young woman narrowed her eyes. "I don't know how I feel about making our kittens into a sideshow."

"Are these *your* kittens?"

"*Our* kittens—they belong to the rescue society."

"I will give them a good home," said Sonia. "They will be very well treated."

"With chickens?" said the young woman.

Sonia bit her lower lip until it hurt. Then she said: "Let me speak with your manager."

The young woman nodded knowingly. "Sure. Let me get her. I think she's with the dogs."

With the young woman out of the way, it wasn't difficult finding the kittens. The corridor of cat cages was noisy with yowls, cries, and complaints. Sonia knew what to look for: two tiny calicos nosing quietly at the grill of their cage. "There you are, my little treasures!" She put one blind kitten in each pocket of her coat. The other cats craned their necks after her, some reaching through their cages, pawing the air for her attention: Sonia apologized to the many abandoned cats with a backward glance, then she slipped out the side door.

Two days later, the county sheriff arrested her at work. He was discreet about it. He found her in the lunch room.

Quietly, he said, "Mrs. Danvers, you're going to come down to the station with me right now. We don't have to let anyone else know what this is about, okay?"

She wasn't locked up, but she sat in the interrogation room until the matter was settled: the rescue center would not press charges if she agreed to give the organization a $500 donation. Also she had to return the two kittens.

It was more than humiliating. The next day she returned to work and pretended that she'd been called to the station on a matter concerning her son. Most of her co-workers knew about her troubled son. As shamed as she felt about this lie, she told herself that, in fact, it *did* have something to do with her son. For the first time in years, she was close to finding a way to accommodate Matt, to settle him somehow.

By the week's end she had located 6 kittens. They weren't blind but they were free and the old woman who gave them up was grateful for the relief. Sonia piled them into a large cardboard box that had once held reams of paper. They mewed and scratched at the cardboard as she drove them home. The long drive gave her plenty of time to ponder the possibilities. It seemed the most obvious option was to blind the kittens herself. A horrifying thought but a compelling one nonetheless. She pictured Matt's delight in handling his boxful of blind pets.

There would be complications, of course. Wouldn't people think it suspect that she had found two litters of blind kittens, one right after the other? And then there were the moral questions. When she'd hold up one of the kittens for its feeding and regard the way it would raise its chin in expectation, its sightless eyes staring at the bright dome of the sky, would she be the woman she had one day hoped to be? No, she would not. But how could she have imagined any of this years ago when she was young and single, and—some said—pretty, riding in her then-boyfriend's pick-up truck, the music loud on the radio and the wind in her hair, her prospects as broad and bright as the horizon she was speeding towards?

SAVE THE POOR
DUMB CREATURES

A lot of girls think all you need is looks to do this, but you need smarts too. All of my girls have smarts. In fact, most of them were studious in high school—the awkward girls you'd see on the fringes, a little too tall, all elbows and knees, their smiles too nice for teenagers trying to keep their cool.

I find them online, modeling second-rate clothing or selling discount housewares. They're modestly getting by, unaware of their own potential. They're surprised when I pick them out, and many, poor dears, think I've made a mistake.

I scare them a little because I'm old enough to be their grandmother and nothing happens here without my say. So they stay healthy, they stay out of trouble, and they stay near me, their wide eyes always seeking my nods of approval.

Every shot, I remind them, costs more than their daddy's monthly salary. And it's hard work. I've got a girl, Kelly, in the water now, three handlers holding mirrors over her, another with the sunbrella over the camera, and the shutter-man himself crouched in the shallow waves, his lens cupped with one hand, his other playing with the aperture. He's sweating like a tri-athlete on the last mile.

It must be a hundred degrees out here on the peninsula.

A few locals watch us from the dunes. They're small brown men—we never see women—with eyes so dark you'd think you'd fall in if you looked hard enough. We must be quite a show for them.

"Do they understand what this is about?" I ask Guillermo, our guide.

He shrugs: "They are simple people, señora."

He says the locals—shall I call them "natives"?—are waiting for the turtle run. Any night now the sea turtles, as big around as bistro tables, will clamber onto the beach to lay their eggs, which the natives steal to eat or sell. It's illegal, Guillermo says, but the government hasn't the money to patrol so much sand.

Tourists don't come out this way: it's too hot, too desolate. We caravanned sixty miles in two RVs over rutted roads to get here, a place without cell reception. My main concern now is that the girls don't get stressed. Stress will show up subtly in a shot, like a poorly-tacked hem.

Kelly's my favorite on this shoot because she's not taken with the success of her last swimsuit issue, even though she got more fan mail than the other girls. She's from Florida, where her parents operate an Everglades tour, puttering into the swamp three times a day in a glass-bottom boat. She's simple like that, doesn't expect much from the world, and grateful when she gets attention.

Tanya, an Asian beauty, waits under a beach umbrella nearby, oiling her long legs. She's older, nearly twenty-six, and she thinks she's seen it all.

Then there are the Olin twins, Norwegian beauties who can barely speak English and seem as vacuous as glass vases, but then I remind myself that they dropped out of university to take my offer. They're obedient and hard-working. They will be stars because they convey a guileless sensuality that accommodates the average male viewer's fantasies.

These are fantasies I am paid to picture, of course. And, frankly, it's the worst part of my job. Truly, a painful bore, because the AMV's mind is a dank, unsavory place, so small, so predictable.

"Kelly, honey, keep your rear up," I tell her. "And arch your back a little."

She nods to let me know she hears.

Yves is muttering to himself. His assistant dabs the master's face with a linen handkerchief.

When the shot's done, Kelly drops into the water for a rest.

"No, no," says Yves. (His "no" sounds like "known.") "We must have her dry."

Kelly blinks surprise at him and offers a little pout: "Sorry, Yves."

I bring her a towel. She pats off the water while I brush her blond-streaked hair. These girls are so young, children really. Kelly's hair smells like a handful of flowers in the hot sun. "That's enough," she says, "I feel like a Barbie doll." I pull her hair back, feathering the ends just-so. "It's got to be perfect, Kelly, you know that." I hear her sigh.

She stands patiently, eyes closed, while Terry, the make-up man, brushes blush onto her cheeks. After a few more dabs, he steps back to admire his work: "You're a Monet, honey." He flutters his brush at her. "Priceless." Camping it up.

As I take my place again in the shade of my umbrella, I notice that the natives continue watching us from the dunes nearby. I count five men sitting on their haunches in the hot sun. They wear faded baseball caps, tattered cut-offs, and sweat-stained t-shirts. They look like L.A. street urchins.

I ask Guillermo to send them away. "It can't be good for them to loiter like that in this heat, Guillermo."

"They wait for work," he says. He glances up at the dunes. "You maybe have work for them."

The way he says this, his voice lilting, I can't tell whether or not it's a question.

"I thought they were waiting for turtles."

"Now they wait for work," he says. "Later they wait for the turtles."

"There's no work here, Guillermo. You can see we're self-sufficient."

He's still squinting at the dunes. He's a short man with unruly black hair and a complexion almost as dark as the natives'. He dresses much better than they, however: blue jeans, leather sandals, and a striped polo.

I say: "Give them a few pesos, if that'll help."

"That would not send them away, señora."

I sigh, exasperated, and stare out at the ocean, where Kelly is waving at the camera and smiling. She has beautiful teeth.

Some people think I got into this business to be near the beauty because I'm not a beauty myself. I was a career girl before career girls were fashionable. I can't tell you how men pitied me—the old maid—and how so many women were unkind in their terribly polite way, calling me "sharp" and "ambitious." I think of them now, the men and women whose condescension I endured. They are, in my mind, far, far behind me, as small and indistinct as castaways adrift on the horizon, waving for rescue.

After the day's shoot, the girls frolic in the waves. Yves was hoping for a good sunset but clouds started stacking on the horizon: they look like mountains now, a towering range of blue-black thunderheads.

The Olin twins are splashing at Kelly and Tanya. Delighted, they squeal like children.

"No rough stuff!" I call. "And no swimming!"

Earlier, Guillermo warned us about sharks.

The handlers are busy collecting drift wood for a fire.

Yves—willowy and overly suntanned, a kerchief fluttering from his thin neck—wants somebody to catch fish for dinner, but no one remembered to bring a rod and reel. "But the guide, he can catch something, no?" Yves says.

Guillermo shrugs apologetically. "I am no fisherman, señor."

We've brought plenty of supplies: fresh fruit and vegetables and several coolers of grass-fed beef, which the handlers will grill on propane stoves. I insist that we eat well on the road.

By the time dinner's ready, the night is black and blustery, the stars obscured by clouds, which grumble now and then.

We girls are sitting closest to the fire, our lawn chairs arranged in a circle, the handlers sitting behind us like servants. Which both excites the men and angers them, I'm sure.

The girls only pick at their food, too aware of their weight. "Don't starve yourselves," I tell them.

The men talk and joke among themselves. This is our first night out and they're a little shy of the girls.

When someone tosses another gnarled log onto the fire, the flames flare, sparks drifting upward, and I am startled to see several natives crouched just beyond our circle of light.

I call for Guillermo.

Suddenly he's at my side, kneeling: "Señora?"

"What's with your locals over there, Guillermo?"

He smiles, as if I were a simpleton. "They wait for the leftovers, señora."

"Are you *kidding*?" I picture these people picking over our scraps. How many are there in the darkness? Where do they come from?

"You prefer they do *not* have the leftovers, señora?"

"No, that's not what I mean." His persistent politeness is irritating. I suspect he thinks badly of me. I say, "We could feed them a little more than scraps, don't you think?"

"We cannot *feed* them, señora." He glances back into the darkness. "They would come twice as many tomorrow. And twice as many the next night."

"Good Lord, that won't do." I peer into the night but can't see them now, the fire light having grown dim.

"I will give them the leftovers, señora."

He starts collecting paper plates from those who have finished eating.

I'm not without my sympathies, but I worry that the natives will somehow jeopardize the shoot. And while I can appreciate their plight, I must remind myself that there's nothing I can do for them that will make a difference in their lives. In three days, we'll be gone, the beach will be empty again, and these people will be waiting once more for the turtles or whatever it is they wait for from week to week.

It's the same everywhere we go: profound poverty, desperate locals, impossible situations, innumerable injustices that we can't begin to redress. Always I feel guilty, of course, but must remind myself that this is business. What could I possibly accomplish by involving myself briefly in the politics of a culture I don't know or understand? A clear conscience maybe. But it's fool's gold. Think of all that I would jeopardize—the livelihood of my crew, my girls, myself, the work of the magazine staff who await our return, not to mention the expectations of two million readers.

Exhausted, the girls are oblivious to our uninvited guests, and this is as I'd prefer it. There's no use in giving them too much to think about.

I say, "You girls ready for bed?"

I see Tanya smirk. She says, "Are you going to tuck us in?"

One of the Olin twins burps a little laugh.

"Here we go," I tell them. I shepherd them to our RV, which sits just outside the firelight. I've learned to keep the RV chilled like a refrigerator when on location because—I know this sounds horrible—it really helps preserve the girls better. They are to me like pedigree show cats: high, high maintenance and more delicate than they themselves will ever understand.

The men do as they like with their RV. I never bother them. They'll stay up late, drinking and playing cards, like steelworkers on holiday.

Our RV is as big as a trailer home. It's been customized to allow each girl a fairly spacious closet and her own sink with vanity. As the girls prepare themselves for bed, I talk them down, like a den mother: "You girls did a good day's work. I'm proud of you. I know it's awfully hot out there—I hope you're wearing some screen, otherwise you'll burn despite your tans."

I tell them a story about one model who started peeling so badly from sunburn that we had to unwrap her like a mummy, slowly and painfully stripping off her dried skin. The girls squeal in disgust as I describe the excruciating process. I have scores of stories like that.

As I'm tucking the girls in, I hear the patter of rain on the roof.

"Vass dat?" one of the twins asks.

"Rain," says Kelly. "I really love when it rains." She stares up as if waiting for more: suddenly a crack of thunder breaks over us.

Tanya yelps in fright. She says, "Are we safe in here?"

"Of course we are," I tell her.

But I pause abruptly because I sense that something's not right: outside, somewhere in the distance, I hear whooping—men making wild noises. I tell the girls not to move, I'll be right back. They eye me anxiously.

When I open the door I can't see much beyond the rain, but now and then, on the slope of the beach, I make out the beams of flashlights and the intermittent flares of cameras.

Something's happening down there.

From the RV steps I call for Guillermo. When he doesn't appear, I shout for him. Finally, he trots out of the darkness.

"Señora?"

"What's going on, Guillermo?"

"It is the turtles, señora. They have come!" His eyes are bright with excitement.

In each hand, I notice, he carries something—oblong dusky things as large as avocados.

"Those are eggs," I say.

He holds them up for me to see.

"Oh my God, what's that?" It's Kelly behind me.

"They're turtle eggs," says Tanya. "I heard Guillermo talking about them earlier."

"Turtles?"

"*Sea* turtles."

Guillermo nods yes, yes. "We can fry them for breakfast, if you like. Very tasty."

"Gross!" says Kelly. "How could you?"

"I do not understand," says Guillermo. He frowns dramatically.

"Aren't these endangered animals?" Kelly says. "Like whales and otters and things? How can you steal *their eggs*, their *babies*!" She has pulled on a windbreaker over her shift.

"This has nothing to do with us," I say. "Let's go back inside."

"It does not harm the turtles," Guillermo says. He looks hurt by Kelly's disgust. "We take the eggs as the turtle drops them into the hole she digs."

"That's heartless," says Kelly.

I'm thinking it must be her Everglades upbringing, all those tours into the swamp to observe wildlife.

Tanya says, "We could stop them."

"We *should*," says Kelly.

"Are you girls crazy?" I snap.

Immediately I know that I should try another tack.

The twins are talking hurried Norwegian to one another.

Kelly says, "Like, who's down there, Guillermo?"

"You cannot go," he says. "There are many—how you say—*natives*. They will not allow you to stop them."

"It's food, right?" says Kelly. I see her eyes flare with purpose. "Isn't that what they want, food?"

"You cannot go," Guillermo says again. He's waving his hands as if words have failed him.

"They're hungry, aren't they, these people?" Kelly is staring hard at him, but he won't meet her eyes.

"Do you know these people?" Tanya asks him.

Now he looks up. "I do not know them, señorita, they are strangers. They will not let you stop them."

"We don't know that for sure," says Kelly.

"Don't even think of it," I warn her. "Girls, let's take five. Come inside—I see there's plenty to discuss."

Tanya turns to glare at me. She says, "Make the crew stop."

It's a command, not a request.

I'm trying so hard to keep from shouting, my throat hurts. I tell myself that I've dealt with worse but I can't recall what it might have been. If the girls leave me now, I won't be able to command their respect tomorrow. I am sure of this. And if I give them permission to leave, it means I will be held responsible.

"Even if I made the crew stop," I say at last, "nobody's going to stop the natives."

"We'll just give them what they want," says Kelly. "We'll give them our food." She raises her fine brows at Guillermo: "That's what they want, right?"

He nods finally: *Yes, that's what they want.* How forlorn he looks.

"We have steaks—all kinds of things they'd like," Tanya says.

Now everyone's nodding in agreement, even the twins.

"Girls, *please*," I say. "We've got a long shoot tomorrow."

Kelly says, "Guillermo, can you talk to your people, can you tell them if they return the eggs we'll be glad to give them everything we've got, lots of food and supplies. Can you do that, please?"

"What's to keep them from returning tomorrow to dig up the eggs again?" I ask. Then I let my anger go, like a weighted rope ripping from my hands: "How naive you girls are—don't be *stupid*!"

Kelly looks at me now, as if for the first time, her wide eyes full of wonderment.

She is so young, so beautiful, I am tempted to take her hand, as I would a toddler's, and explain to her what she is doing wrong. But where would I begin?

She turns again to Guillermo: "They'll keep their word, won't they?"

I see him shrug. Quietly he says, "If you give them so much food, they will not remain here, señorita."

"Give them the coolers," says Tanya. "Everything!"

"Excellent!" says Kelly.

"Excellent!" the twins echo.

I say: "Guillermo, if you help these girls, you're fired."

He shrugs again, giving me his damnable I-can't-help-it look. "I am sorry, señora."

Within minutes, the girls are dressed and heading to the beach, carrying the coolers between them, with Guillermo—also loaded down—leading the way.

"Girls!" I'm shouting. "*Kelly!*" If there were something in my hand, a jar of body lotion or a hair brush, I would throw it after them. "Why should they listen to you! Who are you to tell them *anything?*"

Kelly stops abruptly and turns. She looks at me with profound dismay and puzzlement, as if I were something dead drifting past the window of her glass-bottom boat.

Calmly she asks, "Aren't you coming with us?" The others are silent, waiting.

I hear the smack of heavy drops all around me, then a whoop from the beach. I see a camera flash out there like a spot of lightning. I picture the men plucking eggs from the turtles' sandy nests and I feel a thought leave me like a sigh: *these poor dumb creatures, who will save them from their ruin?*

TARZAN, AGAIN

The land of lame nostalgia is littered with once-vital
characters: Tarzan, Dick Tracy, Doc Savage,
to name a few.
—THE NEW YORK TIMES

After Jane left him, Tarzan moved north and found a
house-share in Berkeley. It's a big, seedy place, not far from
Telegraph Avenue, where the Hare Krishnas and the homeless panhandle the college kids. Just recently he read in the
Times, "The land of lame nostalgia is littered with once-vital characters: Tarzan, Dick Tracy, Doc Savage, to name
a few." It's 1999, the cusp of a new century, and he's seen
too much change too fast and, worse, too many versions of
himself played too poorly. It's been humiliating.

Tarzan has custody of Boy because Jane is in L.A., trying to land a spot on a game show that features a rotating
panel of marginally notable character actors and "personal-
ities." She looks good enough still to be recognized on the
street as the fetching woman who once posed for the cover

of *LIFE*, wearing a tight-fitting leopard skin as she peered with caution from the massive branch of a baobab tree.

Some mornings, as he makes his "silverback latte" in the messy kitchen of his shared house, Tarzan pictures Jane—she never wore leopard—as she would stare wistfully into the jungle from the balcony of their then-happy tree house. At moments like that, she seemed lost in time, a sylph he'd come upon in the early morning mist. It makes him smile to think that he frightened her the first time he dropped from a tree to greet her, this blinding beauty from civilization. She wore an impossibly white blouse and khaki jodhpurs with calf-high lace up boots, her brunette hair mussed and corkscrewed from humidity. She looked so stunning, she frightened him, though he fought hard to hide it. What did he know of women? She was lost, having wandered from her father's party. And wasn't that just like her, to wander?

Her father had been a dreamer and spent decades searching for the Elephant Graveyard and its treasure of piled-high ivory, which, in the end the old man found but refused to betray even as his once-trusted foreman tortured him with a commando knife. Tarzan imagines— still, regularly, incessantly—arriving ten minutes sooner and saving his yet-to-be father-in-law. The scene plays over and over in his head, like one of his Hollywood rehearsals, the director scolding, "This has got to look *real*, man. Don't glance at the camera!" With a flu-like ache deep in his chest, Tarzan realizes that life after forty is too much about wishing to do things over because he is convinced he could do it all better.

This morning, Saturday, he takes Boy to the redwooded trails of the Berkeley hills. The shaded trails smell of loam and minty eucalyptus. It's not jungle but it will do.

Tarzan says, "You feel like swinging a little?"

Boy showed remarkable aptitude for vines at an early age.

Now Boy wants to shave his head and be Goth like his friends at Berkeley High. He's wearing a little foam headset plugged into his Walkman music player, so loud Tarzan hears it hissing into the boy's head from several feet away. But he dare not say anything because Boy would only roll his eyes and grimace at him. That kind of dismissal can send Tarzan into a funk for days.

Tarzan pantomimes swinging. He's brought a rope as big around as an anaconda, which he'll tie to large branches for practice. He raises it like an offering. "Yes?"

Boy blinks at him as if waking from a nap. He's wearing a black t-shirt that says, "My name is Brad Majors." His sneakers look like black hiking boots. His black jeans sag in a way that makes the boy look younger and, sad to say, pathetic.

Tarzan wears a loose-fitting nylon track suit, the only thing he feels comfortable wearing these days.

The problem is, Boy won't talk about his grief. Shortly after the studio rejected Tarzan's last pitch, Cheeta was run over by a drunk driver while crossing the street, just three paces behind Boy and Tarzan. A bloody, horrible scene. And, again, Tarzan blames himself: he should have been mindful of his retinue. L.A. is a jungle. But he was distracted. He just wasn't tracking things well. He wasn't *all there*. For days after the accident, he'd walk into the dewy courtyard of their charming, 1920s hacienda-style apartment complex at dawn and he'd inhale deeply to get his bearings: but there were no bearings. He couldn't smell anything but car exhaust. Maybe that's when his depression started in earnest.

That too-sunny afternoon of the accident, with traffic stacking up behind them, and a crowd congealing on the sidewalk, Boy held Cheeta's limp body, like so many scenes the two had played on the sound stage. It was frighteningly unreal, life imitating art. Maybe that's why Boy didn't cry. At first Tarzan thought this a good thing. Tough boy! But, then, he reconsidered: had he been too hard? Had he shut Boy down?

That night Tarzan wept so loudly, Boy padded to the threshold of the bedroom and gently shut the door on him. Jane had been gone for nearly a month by that time.

The next morning, plugged into his music player, Boy ate his oatmeal in silence and never said a word about Cheeta.

"We loved him so much," Tarzan said.

Then: "It's going to take a while to adjust."

Then: "It's all right to talk about him. It's all right to cry."

But Boy didn't talk about him. Boy didn't cry. That was three months ago.

Now, hefting the rope, Tarzan says, "You like Spider-man, right?"

Boy shrugs. "I don't read comics anymore."

Tarzan is surprised—and gratified—that Boy can hear him through the noise of his earphoned music.

"But Spiderman is cool," Tarzan says. Then, when Boy just stares up at him blankly, he adds, "I mean, it's cool how outside he is, totally misunderstood and not exactly a super-hero, right?"

Boy stares at him blankly.

Tarzan, feeling tiny bullets of sweat speed down his ribs, rushes to fill the void: "I mean, it's not enough to be a hero anymore, you've got to be a *super* hero, right? It's getting silly, isn't it? Or you've got to be an android like the Terminator! Or Robocop!"

Tarzan shakes his head in disgust, then looks away because he's speaking too loudly and he knows his son thinks he's a clueless geezer and he can't stand to see Boy's dismay. They are near the top of the hill, the East Bay laid out below like a toy village. In the sunny distance, the green bay is flecked with white sails. Though an excellent swimmer, Tarzan is terrified of deep water. The jungle is nothing compared to the ocean and its fathomless bottom. Every time Tarzan stares at the water, he thinks of bug-eyed fish that live in total darkness, their mouths as big around as beach balls and grilled with tendril-like teeth.

When he returns his gaze to Boy, Tarzan sees Boy staring into the distance and he wonders what Boy might be dreaming. He must have dreams. Last week, Boy came home with a sky-high ACT score of 32. That's Ivy League level! But Boy has no extra-curriculars. No volunteer work. No hobbies he can boast of. That's why coming here on Saturdays is so important. Tarzan is trying to kick-start something inside Boy: if Boy swung triumphantly thirty yards across the forest, he might take stock, he might stand taller.

Just five-foot-four, Boy is a full foot shorter than Tarzan. Tarzan fears the difference between father and son embarrasses the boy. Why did Boy never grow to his father's stature? Then, with a flush of secret humiliation, Tarzan remembers that Boy is *adopted*. It gives him a pang in the pit of his stomach, like remembering that Jane won't be home when he returns. Sometimes he forgets. Then he worries that Boy carries genes that may lead him to dead-end pursuits. Would Tarzan's own genes have delivered Boy to a better end?

You could be anything! he wants to tell his Boy.

A 32 on the ACT!

He motions to boy to take off the headset.

Reluctantly, Boy does so, the music spewing as loudly as a dowsed campfire.

"Humor me," Tarzan says. "I want to try for a super swing. You remember that one when you were five, hanging on my back?"

Boy shakes his head doubtfully. Their long-ago life in the jungle is receding from Boy's memory like a childish dream. Not even Tarzan pretends that they could go back. But Tarzan remembers everything, even the early joy of clinging to his own ape father's massive back as they hurtled through the jungle canopy, birds bursting from them on every side in explosions of color and song.

Just last week he got an email from his former agent who wrote, "FIY, T. Somebody's bought your name on the internet: Tarazan.com. Sorry, man. We should've seen that coming. They'll sell for $10K if you're interested."

"Yeah," says Tarzan, "wait till Y2K hits, then we'll see."

"What are you talking about?" Boy asks.

Tarzan feels his ears burn. He didn't realize he was talking to himself. "I'm thinking about Y2K," he says. "It's gonna be a mess."

Boy half-shrugs. "It's hippo shit, Dad."

"What's hippo shit?"

"Y2k ain't gonna happen. It's just hype." Boy says this with admirable certainty.

"I guess I've been hyped then."

"*Duped* is the word," says Boy.

Jane taught Tarzan English. How he adored her patience, the way she cupped his chin with one hand to help him enunciate. And still he hates using articles. It was so easy back then: "Jane don't go!" "Tarzan love Jane!" "Jane fuck Tarzan?"

She taught him more dirty words than she'll admit.

Years later, after the movie company refused to renew his contract and Jane was working cameos to help make their rent, she yelled at him: "You're such a *throwback*!"

She meant this as an insult. That's what stunned him. Everything good about him, everything that had made him a millionaire early on, everything that people had once loved, was wrapped up in his being a throwback!

Now he's working with a promoter to market a diet plan that is all about eating like a wild man. It would mean doing the TV commercials himself. He'd have to get in shape. He's been indulging in Dinky Donuts, sometimes as many as a dozen a day.

But, thank God, he can still swing a wicked vine. Even Boy, with his world of distractions, watches him with interest, if not awe. As Tarzan arcs high into the eucalyptus branches, kicking them away with his bare feet, he's tempted to holler loud and long. But he forbears. That's the lesson of the civilized world: keep your cool.

Talk about hippo shit.

Gravity pulls him back with a vengeance. He hurtles to the hillside. This part always gives him chills, his scrotum tightening like a tiny fist. He imagines parachutists feel a similar devastating thrill.

He's a world-class athlete. Why can't he remember this when he's waiting for the bus or picking up his unemployment check?

He lands so hard and fast, he springs forward and sprints for several yards before he can stop. Then, with a gulp of air, he straightens himself, careful to stifle his gasp of effort, before he turns back to Boy.

Boy gives him the thumbs up. His approval makes Tarzan's heart collapse with gratitude. Some things still hold!

Boy takes up the rope, having tucked his music player into his back pocket. Before Tarzan can give him a word of advice, Boy is already airborne. Despite his recent weight gain, Boy has enough upper body strength to hold fast. He has superb form, his legs straight out, his toes pointed, his chin up.

Tarzan hears himself utter a whimper-sigh of satisfaction and admiration. If only there were a way to translate Boy's ability into an advantage. A college scholarship. A role on a TV show. Traction: he and Boy need *traction*.

Jane sent Boy a cell phone so that he and she can talk any time he needs to. She's as worried as Tarzan. It was thoughtful of her, he admits, but a cell phone? "Pretty soon everybody will have one," she said. "You'd better get used to it, T."

She mocks his reluctance to join the modern world. But he has his reasons, she knows: Lotto! Not so long ago, the seductive promise of lottery cards made him dizzy with anticipation, the way he had been as a child, perched on a branch as he watched for a nighttime shower of falling stars. That thrill, that wondrous illumination, seemed to be in every Lotto card he purchased. At his worst, he bought over 100 a day. The same naïveté that had enchanted Jane at the beginning made her disdain him in the end. By the time he joined Gamblers Anonymous, he was ruined and Jane was gone.

On the walk back to the house, Tarzan is thrilled that Boy is not listening to his music player. He wants to talk with Boy about important things—he wants to tell him that it's going to be okay, that he's a good Boy, that things will work out. Deep down, Tarzan doesn't really believe this, but he wants to believe it. He wants to believe in all good things for Boy's benefit. But he is afraid of being a bore or overbearing, so he lets the silence settle between them.

Then he thinks: *Yes, this is what works best, a companionable silence.*

"How about a samosa?" he says when they reach the university.

"Sure," Boy says.

Vendors crowd the sidewalks on Telegraph Avenue. They sell used record albums and CDs and scented candles and incense and hand-painted coffee mugs and tie-dyed t-shirts and rock posters and home-made jewelry and other inconsequential things that students and tourists might like. Tarzan is carrying his big rope coiled over his shoulder. He knows he must look odd, but Berkeley is crowded with odd people.

The samosa stand is a two-wheeled cart parked at the curb. It's run by a small African man named Smithe, a name he pronounces "Smitty." He wears a beaded skull cap and a dashiki whose pattern looks like the paw prints of a big cat.

He grins and says, "Tarzan and Boy, two of my favorite customers. Good day, Gentlemen!"

His grin seems genuine.

Tarzan reads faces well. That's how he knew, long before she said it, that Jane was done with him. He took her for granted, he'll be the first to admit. He regrets that he failed to treasure her later as he treasured her at the beginning. But this happens to every couple, doesn't it? It's like the wear of a waterfall on a rock. Even the most durable things give way over time.

An excuse, he knows. He's full of them.

Boy orders a lamb samosa. Tarzan orders potato. He's been vegetarian since leaving L.A. He thought he'd feel more energetic but there's been no change one way or the other.

Tarzan loves the warm-baked aroma of the samosa, the crisp sound of the wax paper, the heat and heft of the treat in his large hand.

"That rope you're carrying," Smithe says, "it's as fat as a python, man."

Tarzan takes a bite of his steamy samosa, then nods his head. "Yeah, weighs about fifty pounds."

Jane taught him to eat with his mouth closed. Then to wipe his mouth after he was done.

"Is the rope a new addition to your wardrobe," Smithe asks. "Like you carry it around everywhere?"

"Why would I do that?" Tarzan asks. He wipes his mouth with the wax paper.

"Image building," Smithe says. "It's why I wear this soul patch." He points to his chin. "You've got to have an *ensemble*, big guy."

Tarzan smiles as if this were a joke. But it's not a joke. Image was everything when he was a star. Look at Boy: he's wholly remade himself. Nobody has ever guessed Boy's identity. Tarzan, on the other hand, has the bearing of a man who once mattered. People take notice. Sometimes they insist on an autograph, even when they don't know who he is exactly.

Oh, yeah, Tarzan! Wow! Whatever happened to him?

Farther down Telegraph, Boy stops to look at some CDs. Tarzan leans over to pet the vendor's ratty little dog: a Chihuahua. These seem to be popular now. Women carry them like fashion accessories. This dog looks old. It barks its small cough of a bark. Barks and barks and barks. Tarzan reaches down with one finger to pet the dog. He is masterful with animals. He expects the little dog to calm down the moment his finger touches its hot little head. He nuzzles its wet button of a nose. Then, with the speed of a mouse trap's snap, the dog bites the tip of his finger. Hard. With its tiny razor-like teeth. Tarzan recoils with a jolt and a yelp. He whips the air to abate the pain.

"Sweet Jesus!" he says.

Still hopping in pain, he feels something give way: the soft heap of rope slips from his shoulder, slides speedily down his arm, and drops coil after coil on top of the dog. And abruptly there's no more barking. It happens so quickly, Tarzan steps back, startled. It's like a magic act—his rope has buried the dog!

"What the fuck!" the vendor says. He's one of those scruffy young men with a sunburnt face and dirty fingers, so close to homelessness he might as well be begging with an upturned hat in hand.

Tarzan grabs at the rope and Boy helps but it takes longer than it should and when, at last, they have uncovered the dog, Tarzan sees the animal curled in a ball, not crushed but smothered. As inert as a woman's winter muff.

"OH MY FUCK-ING GOD!" the vendor hollers. "YOU FUCKING KILLED MY DOG!"

Tarzan's vision blurs for a moment and he thinks of Jane's father, knifed in the jungle before Tarzan could save him. Then Cheetah splayed bloodily across the asphalt. Tarzan lays a hand on Boy's shoulder to steady himself. Vertigo! He feels the heat of Boy's body, maybe shame burning through Boy's shoulders. Tarzan opens his eyes. The vendor has fallen to his knees. He is wailing over his pet's ratty little body.

A voice in Tarzan's head says, *Now, Tarzan, now!*

Tarzan snatches up the dog, then cupping the animal in both hands, presses his face to its fur, sniffing, listening. He hears no heartbeat. Quickly, efficiently, he pries open the tiny snout, meets it with his lips, then, holding a finger over the dog's still-wet nostrils, he breathes into the animal.

"What the FUCK!" the vendor wails. "Get AWAY!" He claws at Tarzan.

But Boy steps between him and Tarzan, one hand against the vendor's heaving chest. "Wait," Boy says.

The vendor sputters, breathless, his face contorted with anguish and puzzlement. "Wha th-!"

CPR on such a small animal feels nearly impossible, like swimming a straight line against a strong current. But then Tarzan catches the rhythm of the slow, careful work. He imagines oxygen fueling the dog's blood, synapses jerking awake its raisin-sized brain, nerve endings tingling.

Then, like a spark igniting a fire, the ratty little dog hiccups and bucks. Abruptly, it rights itself in Tarzan's massive hands. The dog looks around, blinks, then barks, as if to announce, *I'm back!*

With a gasp, the vendor lunges forward and gathers his dog in both hands, then buries his face in the now-wriggling animal: "My god my god my god my god!" he blubbers.

Tarzan motions for Boy to walk on. They walk in silence for several blocks. Tarzan does not look back. Then Boy says, "That was freaky."

"I'm sorry," Tarzan says.

"You've got nothing to be sorry about!" says Boy.

"You're kind to say so, Boy."

"It was an accident! The dog's alive!"

"I should have been more careful," Tarzan says. "I haven't been careful."

"Shit happens," says Boy.

"No," says Tarzan. "People *make* shit happen when they're careless."

Hearing this, Boy seems to settle into a sulk. Then, as they arrive at the house, he says, "You don't have to be so hard on yourself, Pop."

Tarzan nods okay, because he doesn't want to say more than he has to and he's already said enough. He's grateful for what seems to be a break in the clouds of Boy's mood.

Later, his bloodied finger bandaged, he makes Boy's favorite breakfast for supper—a sunnyside up on fried toast, called "toad in a hole." He turns to watch Boy squeeze fresh oranges for juice. Boy is wearing his earphones again, the music hissing from his head.

Tarzan buys oranges by the case at the Oakland wholesale market once a week. He has to get up before dawn for the errand. It's one of his favorite things to do. He loves how the city streets are nearly empty at that hour and the world has yet to crowd and elbow itself into his life. He loves striding though the messy aisles of produce, the sellers calling out their bargains, the air grassy sweet with the smells of fruits and vegetables. He has offered to take Boy before school one day, but Boy isn't a morning person. It's all Boy can do to get out of the house in time to skateboard the six blocks to Berkeley High and still he's late half the time.

Soon, he'll be gone to college or trade school. Tarzan promises himself that his own life will be on track by that time. He fantasizes about living in one of those cool custom tiny homes made from a shipping container, maybe up the coast somewhere. He'd like a pet. Not a chimp. No, never again a chimp. But *some kind* of furry friend.

At the thought of Cheeta, he swallows hard to keep down his grief. He spatulas the eggy toast in the skillet to distract himself, then feels a wave of regret snatch him up and tumble him in memories. But, before Boy notices, he talks himself out of it or thinks he does: *Boy still swings great. And he scored 32 on the ACT! The new agent says Tarzan's Wild Man diet can't fail! Y2K is hippo shit! The new century will be a good one, maybe even a better one!*

Then he sees Boy looking at him with concern, the way he might watch a river for crocodiles. "Hey," Boy says. "What's up?"

Tarzan's smile is like a shrug. He is amazed that Boy can hear him through the noise of his music. Then, because the day has gone so well, he offers a confession he hasn't offered in a month or more: "I miss Cheeta, don't you?"

Boy pauses, one orange half in hand, then looks out the kitchen window, east to the Berkeley hills, where the sky is as deep a blue as his mother's eyes. He's nodding in agreement. He says, "Yeah, Dad, Cheeta."

SAMUEL'S SECRET

When Bo and his wife, Sara, bought a forty-acre farm just west of Spokane, Bo insisted to friends and acquaintances that it wasn't on account of safety. No, they were not afraid of living in the city. They *loved* the city. Still, Bo pointed out, "You have to be vigilant in the city. Always *on watch.*" He was careful not to say "on guard." After nearly twenty years of living downtown, in a broad-shouldered "shingle style" house he and Sara had restored to its original splendor—featured in the paper's lifestyle section and in *Spokane Magazine*—he admitted to himself that the city now felt too claustrophobic.

Walkers in their city neighborhood let their dogs shit in his tree wells. Panhandlers accosted him as soon as he stepped out to the street: "'Cuse me? Can I ask you a question?" Commuters parked their cars in front of his garage. Despite his pleas and protests, the city police would never come to ticket, much less tow. If he left the gate open to his brick-walled back yard, somebody would wander in—

sometimes a sightseer, sometimes a vagrant. He couldn't count how many garden spades and lawn chairs he had lost to petty thieves over the years. Every day, the mail slot of his old house's beautifully tall, historic doors was choked with civic announcements, candidate flyers, coupons, and carry-out menus. And there was always a salesperson or a pollster or a volunteer for some good cause ringing his front bell, then peering through the thick glass, as if it were obvious that Bo was hiding inside. It seemed the world was pushing in like cows herding into a feed pen.

Sara felt it too. She no longer tended their small, award-winning front yard, with its thicket of rose bushes, because if she wasn't being entreated by panhandlers, she was having to stop her work to talk with neighbors and passersby. She wanted to be polite, she *needed* to be civil, she considered herself a nice person. She was, after all, a social worker.

For the longest time, Bo answered her complaints with a shrug. It was only natural that passersby would make comments and ask questions about their beautiful house. How could Bo and Sara refuse their interest and good will?

On twenty-four acres, Bo and Sara couldn't even *see* their nearest neighbor. Every morning before breakfast, Bo stepped out of the kitchen and peed into the grass beside the smoke house. He could have walked around naked every day and nobody would know. He wondered, Would the novelty of such freedom ever grow old?

No way.

When friends and acquaintances heard of their move, it seemed every one of them was envious, even jealous. Bo and Sara had a big barn and several other outbuildings, including a large chicken house. None of it was in good repair. In fact, they had overpaid for this neglected potato farm. As the land was "in agricultural conservation," they couldn't sell any of it to developers. It had to be farmed. Bo wished he had done more research about all of this. He knew nothing about farming. Maybe an apple farm would have been easier.

Still, he and Sara were the objects of envy because they happened to buy the farm just six months before the Covid-19 pandemic. Sara could do her social work counseling online through Telehealth. Bo—recently retired from teaching high school history—had hoped to get income from renting the barn apartment to tourists but the apartment wasn't in great repair and it didn't seem like anybody was interested in staying out here anyway, forty minutes from Spokane. When he and Sara reviewed their finances, Bo shook his head in dismay and tried to joke: "Are we fools for dreaming we could be self-sufficient?"

In answer, Sara's expression wasn't exactly panic but it conveyed more than worry. Though she had not said as much, he knew her fear: he would collapse while digging up potatoes or he'd run the tractor into a skunk hole and the machine would roll over on top of him and then Sara would be stranded here, on the brink of bankruptcy.

But already they were selling most of their eggs every week. They had expanded their garden to put themselves in the produce business. And they had acquired eight barn cats, two farm dogs, and fifty-six chickens, which the dogs guarded every night. They wanted sheep and goats too and maybe turkeys and pigs. Big plans! Bo told himself they weren't too old to run after such dreams. That is, they weren't *old* old. But now, as he and Sara flirted with ruin, he admitted to himself that his dream of restoring a decrepit farm was nothing more and nothing less than his race against inevitable ill health and his last days: a grand challenge to prove to the world that he was not done yet.

And then the pandemic. It was just bad luck. It scared Bo because there was no way he could afford to be sick, even if he might survive the virus.

So, he came up with a plan: he would invite Samuel, his brother—a rich widower—to shelter at the farm. He and Sara would spoil him and he would grow to love the place, then maybe he would invest in their dream. Samuel could have the barn apartment and fix it up anyway he pleased. But Bo had never been close to Samuel, in part because Samuel was seven years his junior, but also because Samuel had led a sedate and privileged life, the husband of a successful jeweler. Bo had long thought Samuel a slacker—a man with little ambition or imagination: a "weenie." Until Evelyn's coronary eighteen months ago, he hadn't talked to Samuel in years.

But, too, Bo was all Samuel had. Their parents were long dead.

Samuel arrived in a late model Lexus. A corkscrew of dust unfurled behind him as he sped down the gravel lane. He had always driven too fast. A tall, wan man with heavily lidded eyes and a thick mane of raven-colored hair, he seemed almost a stranger to Bo. He didn't remember his brother dying his hair black. Samuel looked ten years younger than his fifty years. His finely-tailored slacks and suede jacket must have cost more than Bo made in a month. The pronounced lump under his jacket Bo recognized as a pistol. Samuel had a permit for conceal carry because Evelyn had owned a jewelry store. It had always seemed a joke, his timid, little brother carrying a pistol. But now he didn't like its suggestive bulge.

Bo waved a greeting but held back. "Samuel, where's your mask?"

He and Sara had been careful, even when the propane delivery woman came by. They each wore a custom, all-cotton mask and kept extras in the truck's glove compartment.

Samuel turned his head in puzzlement. "Why do I need a mask?"

Bo heard a small moan from Sara, beside him. He said, "Samuel, we don't know where you've been. Haven't you been wearing a mask?"

Samuel shrugged. "It's just a flu, Bo. No big deal."

Bo could feel the blood rise to his face, the tips of his ears suddenly hot. "Half the country is in lockdown, we've got over a hundred thousand dead, and you think it's like the fucking flu?"

"With all due respect to the dead and dying, Bo, those people were sick to begin with. You and me are healthy. And we're not *that* old."

Bo would be 67 in December. Since buying the farm, his blood pressure had risen by thirty points. He was pre-diabetic and there was also incipient asthma when the weather grew warm, as it was now. He hid his wheezing from Sara but maybe she knew. Just recently she had started taking medication for anxiety.

Sara said, "Samuel, dear, you may think lightly of the pandemic but you're no expert, are you? For all you know, you could be a carrier."

Samuel half-shrugged and seemed to stifle a smirk "Whatever, Sara. I'll wear a mask if that will make you guys happy."

Bo fetched a mask from the truck—one of those blue cheapies. But at least it was something. He held it out to his brother.

Samuel took it without enthusiasm, then smiled at them like a con man: "What time's dinner?"

Later, before supper, Bo anticipated with dread Samuel's inevitable complaints—the apartment was too hot, the floors too dusty, the toilet too old, on and on. Samuel had been spoiled from the start. When he was six, he ate almost nothing but cereal for an entire year.

Entering the house, Samuel said, "It's so nice to be in this little hideaway." As promised, he was wearing his mask. Sara sat him at the end of their long farm table.

"You can take that off to eat," she said.

He glanced up at her mischievously: "Really?"

"We're so happy you're here!" said Bo. He coached himself to go easy. He didn't want to sound too patronizing.

"After dessert, we'll give you a tour," Sara said. She smiled her beatific smile. When she and Bo first met, Bo had joked, "Your angelic smile doesn't fool me," and then Sara looked a bit shaken. She took herself that seriously.

"I can't walk in the grass," said Samuel.

"Allergies?" Sara asked.

"Snakes." Samuel offered an awkward smile. "I'm deathly afraid of snakes."

Bo squinted at his brother as if to get him in focus: "Samuel, I never knew that!" How had he grown so distant from his only brother? Maybe Bo had been too self-absorbed, too judgmental, too quick to assume Samuel didn't care?

"The snakes are harmless," Sara said. "They eat the mice."

"Even so," Bo said, "you won't see them in the grass—"

"Exactly!" said Samuel.

"I mean, they're nocturnal mostly and very secretive."

Bo did not mention that he and Sara sometimes found black snakes in their basement. The snakes lived in the crevices of their old stone foundation. One was five feet long.

"I'll get some snake boots," Samuel said.

"What are snake boots?" Bo asked.

"Rubber, up to your knees," he said. "That way, if the snake bites you, it will be repelled."

"By the rubber?"

"That's right."

"Is this what snake hunters wear?" Sara teased.

"Who sells snake boots?" asked Bo.

"They're not marketed as *snake boots*," said Samuel. "And I wish you two would stop making fun of me."

"We're not making fun," said Bo. "It's just that there aren't any venomous snakes in Washington, little brother."

"Well," said Sara, "with the exception of rattlers."

"Little rattlers," said Bo. "They hide under rocks."

"Nobody dies from their bite," said Sara.

Samuel winced at the thought: *"Nobody?"*

"They're little snakes, like I said!" Bo pinched two fingers together as if to show their miniscule size.

"Well, they're a little bigger than that," Sara said with a chuckle.

Samuel offered a chuckle of his own. "I'm much reassured now!"

Later, in bed with Sara, Bo said: "We need to lighten up. Did you have to mention rattlers?"

"Sorry, babe, but Samuel will never agree to stay here. Isn't that obvious?"

Bo understood that this was ever-practical Sara talking. She overestimated a challenge in order to spare herself the disappointment. Sometimes he wondered what in him she had overestimated. Was she disappointed now?

"Where else is he going to go?" Bo asked.

"A rich widower can go wherever he pleases. Florida?"

"Doesn't Florida have more snakes than anyplace in America?"

"This isn't about logic, babe."

But neither was home ownership or, in this case, farm ownership. Bo never imagined he'd be desperate to possess a farm. But here he was, scheming to net his brother's help to realize a dream Bo had never imagined he himself would ever desire.

Two days later, while Sara was feeding the chickens, Bo stopped by the barn to bring Samuel five warm bran muffins. He found the apartment locked. After some pounding, he roused his brother, who peered tentatively through a crack in the foyer door. Stepping finally to the glass entry door, Samuel took some time undoing the door's three locks.

"I didn't know we had *three* locks on this door!" Bo said.

"I called the locksmith in yesterday," Samuel said matter-of-factly. "He put in two."

Bo stepped back because his brother was maskless. "Samuel, we're safe here."

"The locks make me feel safer, Bo."

"If anybody were to come onto the property," said Bo, "the dogs would raise an alarm."

"And then what?" said Samuel.

Bo stared at his brother in pained disbelief. Samuel had been three days on the farm.

The next morning, as Bo was putting on his boots after breakfast, Sarah said, "My god, Bo, your brother cares nothing about Covid-19 but he's worried about what? Thieves?"

Bo shrugged, stood, then stepped to the kitchen window as if to see Samuel in the barn apartment, a good distance from the house: "Some people are like that."

"Was he always?"

"No," he said. "As a kid, he seemed happy and normal to me, though Mom and Dad spoiled him."

"Has he ever been mugged?" Sarah asked. "Assaulted?"

"Not that I know of. His marriage seemed good enough, don't you think?"

"Well, they had no children."

She and Bo had two boys, grown now. Both had visited that first Christmas and pronounced the farm "awesome" but showed little interest in its operation. Maybe in another few years? Bo wondered.

"I don't know if she and Evelyn tried to have children," he said. "And I don't know if Samuel cared all that much."

"Well, what does he care about?"

"He plays a lot of online bridge."

When Bo went out to fetch the dogs—a Corgi and a Lab, named Frick and Frack— he couldn't find them. He was perplexed because they weren't likely to stray. They were always at his heels when he fed the chickens. After checking the hens, Bo returned to the barn and knocked on Samuel's door. When Samuel appeared, there were Frick and Frack, circling his brother, tails wagging fiercely, nosing the door, jawing at Samuel's knees.

"Samuel, those aren't house dogs. They belong out here."

"They seemed lonely," he said. He wore a big terry-cloth robe that might have belonged to Evelyn. He was also wearing rubber waders that stopped just short of his knees. No mask, as usual.

The dogs nosed the glass door, eager to get at Bo. Any sensible person would have seen that these dogs were getting frantic.

At last Bo snapped: "Let them out!"

When Samuel opened the door a crack, both dogs butted through, nearly knocking Bo over as they ran to the grass.

Bo righted himself, then said, "The next time you get an urge to put in another lock, will you call me?"

"I have a right to feel safe, Bo."

"I'm not arguing," he said. "I'd just like to know what's going on."

"You weren't around."

"I do have work to do, have you noticed?"

"Then get on with it, don't let me stop you!"

Bo swallowed a sigh, then regarded his brother watching

him in his smirky little brother way. Bo didn't know what Samuel wanted. Maybe nothing. Maybe everything. Surely grief was riding him hard.

"Do you need anything?" Bo asked. "Shall we take you out later?"

"Where, to that godforsaken little town?"

"There's an ice cream shop."

"The Cow" specialized in old-fashioned soft-serve. The little shop looked like it had been there for fifty years. Always there were long lines at both windows. Bo ordered the same cone every time: chocolate-dipped vanilla. Sara's usual was a chocolate and vanilla twist. Samuel got a sundae.

"You can't eat all that," Bo said.

They were standing in the parking lot, a safe distance from each other.

Samuel held up his sundae like a taunt. "Jealous?"

"Plenty jealous," said Bo. "You're lucky your indulgences haven't caught up with you."

"Samuel, you've managed to keep your figure!" Sara teased.

"It's worry that keeps the weight off."

"What do you have to be worried about?" Bo said. He checked himself. He was angry, he realized.

"Everybody has worries," Sara said diplomatically.

Samuel laughed. He seemed nervous. "If only you knew!"

"*Do tell*," said Bo, still irritable.

"I'm worried about *you two*!" Samuel waved his tiny plastic spoon at them. "Here you've taken on a broken-down farm when you should have invested in a quiet retirement."

99

"The farm is plenty quiet," said Bo. "And it's not so broken."

Samuel raised his brows. "Could've fool me, brother."

Later, in bed, Sara said, "Do you think Samuel was carrying his gun tonight?"

Sara had an open book in her lap. It took her months to read a book in bed because, within minutes, she'd be asleep.

"Samuel always carries his gun, Sara."

"Remind me again: when did that start?"

"He claimed he needed a gun because he often transported jewels for the store."

"But he hasn't shot anybody."

Bo shrugged, then slid into bed: "Not yet."

It was nearly dawn when dog howls woke him. He threw on his robe and jumped into his untied workboots, then ran to the noise. Mist was rising from the grass, the sun a pink smear beyond the trees. It felt like it would be another hot day.

He found Frick and Frack outside the chicken coop. Frick was howling in grief, it seemed. Frack was yapping in a frenzy, sprinting from one side of the pen to the other.

It took Bo a while to understand what he was seeing: eviscerated chickens, blood and guts, strewn across the chicken yard—a leg here, a head there. He opened the gate, the dogs followed nervously, sniffing first this dead bird, then that one. Frack whined.

"What the fuck!" Bo wailed. All gone: 56 birds. Angrily, confusedly, he wheeled about and glared at the dogs: "Where were you?" Then, shouting: "WHERE THE FUCK WERE YOU!"

The dogs cowered and backed away.

Then he knew.

"It's all my fault!" Samuel was moaning a few minutes later. He stood just inside the kitchen door, wearing the same clothes he'd worn the day before. Gray roots were showing in the part of his thick hair. "I thought the doggies would enjoy one night in—and they did. I *spoiled* them. It made me *feel* better."

"It was probably a coyote and its kits," said Sara. "They can go crazy like that. Easy enough for them to dig under the fence when the dogs are gone."

"I'm so sorry!" Samuel wailed.

"Fifty-six laying hens!" said Bo.

"Fifty-five," said Sara. "I found one hunkered on a rafter, poor thing"

"She'll probably never lay another egg in her frightened life," Bo said bitterly.

"We were selling as many as a hundred eggs a week," said Sara.

Samuel shook his head in anguished disbelief.

"What she's saying," said Bo, "is that we need you to buy us new chickens." When Samuel didn't answer, he added, "As soon as possible."

Samuel grimaced, blinked, bit his lower lip, then wiped one hand across his brow. At last he said, "I can't. I'm broke!"

Then, haltingly, he explained that he had gotten too deep into playing online bridge for money. It was illegal and exhilarating. Sometimes he won, but mostly he lost. In the eighteen months since Evelyn's death, he had run through the entire estate. All he had left was his three-year-old Lexis and a splendid wardrobe. He had used the last of his credit card on installing locks in the barn apartment.

When Samuel returned to the barn, Bo started pacing the kitchen floor. "I didn't know my brother was *crazy*—I just didn't know!" He stopped and looked to Sara. "What are we going to do?"

"He's family," said Sara. "What can we do?"

"We can't afford him," said Bo. "We can't even afford to replace the chickens!" Suddenly he was fighting back tears. He thought of the chickens, the panic of their final minutes, the gory glee of the heartless coyotes—it was too much.

"Sit down," Sara said. "Let me make you some tea."

"With whiskey," he said hoarsely. It was nine o'clock in the morning. He'd been up since five already. He had a raging headache. And his brother was crazy.

At supper time, when Samuel showed up at the screened door, he was wearing his mask. His outfit looked ridiculous—a checkered silk shirt, like something a jockey would wear, and new blue jeans, and his rubber boots. "I brought you something," he said.

Sara said, "Come in, honey. You want a drink?"

"I've been drinking all day," he said.

Sara glanced knowingly to Bo, who had been drinking all day too.

Leaning against the stove, Bo felt woozy and lost. He could hardly predict what would become of him, Sara, and Samuel. Sara was doing social work—via computer—for the county jail. She could have made the same money, with much less stress, as a clerk at Home Depot. But she loved social work. Bo had been contemplating taking a job as a shuttle driver for the state—they needed somebody to transport the elderly to doctors' appointments and so on. For sure he'd get Covid in the process. As he watched Samuel, he wondered if his brother was possibly employable.

Sara said, "I know how upset you must be."

Bo wasn't sure who she was talking to.

Samuel said, "I should just go away!"

"Where would you go?" This was Sara's social work voice.

Samuel grimaced. "I'm such a loser—why would anybody want me around!"

"I don't want to hear it," said Bo. "I cannot abide self-pity. So just cool it!"

"Sorry," he said, "I was only speaking the truth."

"You said you had something?" Sara asked.

"Yes," said Samuel, "and I won't take 'no' for an answer." He fingered something from his shirt pocket: a ring. He set it on the kitchen table.

"Your wedding ring?" Bo said.

"*Engagement* ring," said Samuel. "It's worth enough to buy you some chickens and more."

"You want me to *hock* the frigging engagement ring you gave to Evelyn?" Despite Bo's seeming disbelief, bordering on outrage, already the notion of selling the ring was turning in his head.

"You could sell it online," Samuel said. "There's a good market for rings like this. It's antique. Platinum with rose diamonds. I can give you a certificate of authenticity. As you may know, there's a lot of crooked dealing online."

"Are you making a pun?" Sara asked.

After a moment, Samuel got the joke and laughed. "No, I'm serious!"

Bo took his brother's right hand as if to shake it but instead held it fast. He said, "You've got to promise us you're through with gambling."

Already he was feeling better. Abruptly, he decided his brother wasn't contagious. Crazy maybe, but not contagious.

"I didn't set out to gamble," said Samuel. "I love bridge— you know how much I love it!"

"Yes," said Bo, "you love bridge."

In bed that night, Sara said, "I think counseling would help."

Bo fought off his damp socks. "And who's gonna pay for that?"

"It comes from depression," said Sara. "Ever since Evelyn's heart attack, he's been in a free-fall. I think that much is clear."

Bo stared at the ring, now on his nightstand. "How much could this thing be worth?"

Twenty-seven thousand dollars, according to a jeweler in Spokane. He offered Bo and Sara two-thirds of that. They took it. Driving home, Bo said, "I bet that ring is worth twice what he quoted us."

"Doesn't matter," said Sara. "Now we can get back to business. Maybe some counseling for Samuel?"

"He probably won't think he needs it."

Much to their surprise, Samuel *liked* counseling and "went" once a week via his smart phone. Bo figured they had funds enough to pay for six months of counseling. Samuel was now even willing to walk in the grass . . . if the cats would join him. He threw cat kibble before him, then let the cats chase after it. His new medication had made him livelier and bolder.

Now, watching Samuel walk into the field where Bo hoped to plant corn next season, Bo called: "Hey, bro."

When Samuel turned to greet him, Bo saw that he had cat kibble in both hands. Several of the barn cats were rooting through the grass nearby.

"It's lovely out here, isn't it?" Samuel said. He was wearing yet another pair of new blue jeans, a white turtle neck under a bright blue V-neck sweater. And those rubber boots. He had tied a blue polka-dotted bandana around his neck. His hair, freshly dyed, was tar black.

There was something different about him. It wasn't simply the medication. Was it that he had somehow given in or given up? His eyes wouldn't quite meet Bo's. Samuel seemed inclined to gaze above him, to the fast-moving clouds.

"I never imagined I'd live in the country," Bo said. He couldn't remember the last time he had talked earnestly with his brother.

"Yes." Samuel offered a smile that seemed patronizing. "You surprised me."

"Really?" Bo had assumed his brother never gave him a second thought. "What did you expect?"

"Not this," he said. "Not out here. You have no neighbors!" This didn't sound like a criticism.

"We have neighbors," said Bo, "they're just farther away."

"Do you mix with them? Do they know you?"

"We don't have time for that. You see what we're into."

Samuel smiled at him sadly. "When you were a boy, you wanted to be a chef and run a chain of restaurants."

"Did I?" Bo remembered only history capturing his interest when he was fifteen, in Mrs. Boswell's class. "I recall that I wanted to be a lot of things."

"But not a farmer. Never a farmer."

A breeze made the knee-high grass undulate.

"But isn't that a great thing?" said Bo. "If life doesn't offer us a surprise now and then, what's the point?"

"Oh," said Samuel, "so the point is to wait for the surprise?"

"Sure, both good and bad." Bo watched the grass for a moment, then said: "I know it's been tough for you since Evelyn's—passing. But you're young still."

This made Samuel laugh a boyish laugh. "Young?"

"To me, everyone seems young," Bo joked. Then he hurried on: "I mean, don't you want an *occupation*, something that might give you perspective?"

Samuel sighed, then tossed more kibble to the cats. The big orange tabby was wending through and around Bo's legs.

Samuel looked in Bo's direction but not quite at him: "I know you need money, Bo. I see this place is eating you up—"

"I wouldn't say that."

"No, you wouldn't. But I can see how it weighs on you. I'm sorry, I don't mean to make you feel defensive."

"I'm not defensive!" Then, when he saw Samuel grimace slightly, Bo laughed at himself: "I'm a *case*, aren't I?"

"You've always been stubborn and kind of dunderheaded." He said this kindly but nonetheless it hurt a little.

"It's the historian in me," he said. "This farm is a piece of history. Established in 1860. And I have a chance to bring it back the way we brought back that city house."

"You don't need to explain, Bo. I get it."

"This could be your home too."

"Look at me. What good would I do you?"

"You're my brother!"

"Yes, we're brothers!" Samuel was teasing him.

"I'm serious!"

"I know you are! But let's stop shouting!"

Bo wanted to tell him that, after their parents died, he had a recurring dream that he was adrift on an ice floe—and in the near distance behind him, in the direction he was drifting, he could hear the rumble of a waterfall. He had felt that alone. But now, considering all he could say to his brother, he decided against getting dramatic. It was clear that Samuel wasn't going to stay.

He said, "Just when it seems we're getting to be friends, you're going to leave me."

"The loss is mutual, Bo."

When Samuel turned to toss the last of the kibble, Bo saw that he had tucked his pistol beneath the waistband of his jeans—just behind his right hip, as if to make himself ready for a fast draw.

Two days later, Bo was pouring fuel into his tractor when a white American four-door glided down the gravel drive. He walked out to greet the strangers. A man and a woman, thirty-somethings, dressed casually, as if going to Walmart. Every now and then somebody would show up like this, lost or curious.

The woman seemed to smile kindly behind her maroon cloth mask. The man nodded the way a passing farmer would. She was taller than he and wore a cheap blue blazer, like a bank clerk, but she wasn't a bank clerk. She had the shrewd eyes of an IRS auditor: her eyes were everywhere, appraising every little thing. The young man, stocky and thick in the middle, might have been a wrestler in college. His brown blazer fit tightly: maybe nothing fit him right. He had a buzzcut and wore gold, wire-rimmed eyeglasses. His mask was patterned with tiny yellow ducks.

He said his name was Chad. Hers was Miranda.

When they introduced themselves as U.S. Marshalls, Bo tried to laugh—he was suddenly nervous. He ended up coughing. As he tried to recover, he held up one finger, as if to say, "Wait, just wait." He had a foreboding that this was no joke.

At last he croaked, "Is this about my *brother*?"

Chad nodded yes. Then Miranda explained that there was little they could say other than to let him know that Samuel was gone and would not be returning. But he was fine.

Bo swung around as if to see through the barn to his brother's apartment, even though he knew that Samuel had gone out this morning to run an unspecified errand.

"Wait," he said, turning back, "is Samuel a *criminal*?"

"We wouldn't say that," said Miranda. "Let's say that he was into the ring pretty deeply."

"Ring? What ring?"

"We can't say," said Chad. Then he smiled, announced by the crinkling at the corners of his eyes.

"You just said *ring*. Why can't you say *which* ring?" Bo looked from one to the other. He felt short of breath, tempted to tear off his mask. "You mean some kind of *gambling* ring? Samuel played bridge, for Christsake. You mean some kind of *bridge* gambling ring?"

"We can't say, sir."

"Why did he go away?" Bo said. "Where did he go?"

"Let's say some bad actors wanted to collect a debt."

"Actors?"

"*Bad* actors," said Chad.

"He was in debt to *bad actors*?" said Bo. "When you say he's fine, you mean he's under protection, like the *witness protection program*?"

"We can't say," said Miranda.

"We can only say that you will not see him again," said Chad.

"But he's okay?" Old snapshots of his brother flew through his memory: Samuel at five, waving a lollipop at the camera; Samuel at 8, grinning to show the gap where two baby teeth were missing; Samuel at 12, dressed as a Jedi knight; Samuel at 17, tuxedoed for the senior prop; Samuel at 22, pushing wedding cake into Evelyn's grinning face.

"He'll be fine," said Miranda.

"We've been doing this for a long time," said Chad.

This sounded reassuring but Bo's mind was a dust devil of confusion: they've been *doing what* for a long time? "How do I know *you two* are not the bad actors!" he said.

Miranda gave Bo a business card that announced her name and a cell phone number. "You can check us out."

"And call if you have any more questions," said Chad.

"But you won't answer ANY of my questions!"

"That's right," said Chad. "We've come only as a favor to your brother. He wanted you to know."

"Know *what?*" Bo cried. "What do I know!"

As he watched the car pull away, he shook his head in disbelief. Then he ripped off his mask and shouted, "Assholes!"

Later, at the dinner table, Sara said, "That's why he was so paranoid!"

They were eating carry-out Thai, which, in this part of the county, was pretty bad.

"I'm never going to see my brother again!" Bo had been grieving for hours, stunned by the depth of his loss. How could he have taken Samuel for granted?

"Maybe he's happier now," said Sara. She forked Pad Thai onto Bo's plate. "But what are we going to tell the boys?"

"Like they care? We hardly see them ourselves!"

"Still, they're going to ask."

"Tell them Samuel joined an ashram in Spain—I don't fucking know."

"Things could be worse, babe. Samuel's safe and so are we. I was afraid he was going to shoot somebody by accident."

"He left the gun behind!" said Bo. "I found it on his bed."

"Oh my god!"

"He was wearing that pistol just yesterday in his jeans!"

"We have to get rid of it!" said Sara.

"Let's bury it," he said.

"Where?"

Bo stared down at his food, which he hadn't touched. The thought that he'd never see Samuel again defied all logic. At last he said, "We'll bury it the same place we buried the chickens."

Sara shook her head: "Too messy, babe."

"Then we'll throw it into the river."

"Yes." She took his hand. "That will do."

As days passed, then months, and the pandemic grew and grew, it seemed to Bo that a grave unavoidable threat—like a devastating blizzard—was closing in. Sometimes, early in the morning, he'd wake up gasping until he could take a shot from his inhaler. In all this time, he couldn't bring himself to throw Samuel's pistol into the river. Sara said nothing about it. She kept working at her telehealth. Between clients, she'd stand at the big window and look out at their fields, a cup of tea in one hand. He worried that she was thinking of a life elsewhere.

Bo continued working the farm, now with a third dog to train, much younger than Frick and Frack. He kept Samuel's unloaded pistol on top of the bedroom bureau, like a paperweight. Every week, when he dusted it, he pictured Samuel, with his pricey wardrobe and now a new name, waiting till the pandemic passed and he could sell jewelry at a cut-rate mall store in an eastern town of, say, twenty thousand modest souls, none of whom would think twice about who Samuel was and what he might have done. Bo wanted to believe—he hoped—that Samuel pictured him too, still safe on his farm, with his chickens and dogs and many cats, his days too full of chores and his nights too quiet, Sara sleeping soundly beside him, in an old house well back from the road and perhaps too far from the nearest neighbor.

FAR WEST

News headline, July 12, 2020

*"Arizona man driving stolen vehicle caught with
rattlesnake uranium, whiskey, and firearm"*

We were about twenty miles from Zuni land when the
troopers nabbed us. Could've gotten in on the Arizona side
and then they'd've had to petition for extradition. It's a sovereign nation. But our luck broke bad in Reno, where Marty
Medeiros hung us up for five days as we bargained with him
for a truck. By "bargain" I mean argue. Marty owed me
$2500 for some gold dust I'd traded him, won in a game of
miniature golf—I'm still good with a putter. Marty gave me
27 Liberty-head silver dollars, a Confederate five-dollar bill
that he swore was real (came with authentication certificate),
a sawed-off shotgun, which I hocked as soon as I could, and
a truck. Not the truck we ended up with, though.

Me and SunMist were crashing at his place, which was
kind of a junk yard. Marty was a fabricator and scrap man.

113

He's the one taught SunMist how to weld. She was hardly out of her teens back in those days and Marty was already near thirty. She won't admit it, but I'm pretty sure he took advantage of her. So our connection was kind of messy and Marty wasn't ever one to deal straight, one way or another, anyway. That's how reduced my lot was, that I had to deal with a low-life like Marty Medeiros.

The jailer in Winslow wasn't a trooper. He was a county employee—a skinny nobody with a tidy potbelly and clown-big feet. He stood there, on the other side of the bars, and stared at me for a while. I was sitting on my stainless steel bunk, trying to cool down, a migraine coming on. Just a matter of time before I seized.

I nodded a greeting, tried a smile. Neither one of us was wearing a mask.

He said, "Heard you fed a rattler uranium."

Where do they get these people?

"Yeah," I said, "I've been experimenting. Got me some rattlers fifteen, nearly twenty, feet long back home."

He nodded as if to picture this. Then: "Bullshit."

"They glow in the dark, man. You should see them."

He reached to one side and flicked the overhead light off and on. "They tell me you're epileptic."

I closed my eyes and covered them with both hands.

"I could do this all night," he said.

"Would you?" I said. "Please?"

Just then I heard SunMist vomiting in the next cell.

"Oh, that's just fucking fine," the jailer said in disgust.

I uncovered my eyes.

He left the light on, then went to fetch the Matron.

"Honey bun," I said, "are you passing?"

SunMist groaned: "God. Damn. Devil!"

"Hold on," I said. "I'm here." Like this was supposed to be comforting.

Hearing SunMist's pain—the way she moaned and growled and gasped—gave me the shakes. As bad as watching a dog fight.

"Hey, can we get some HELP here?" I hollered down the hall, pressing my face against the cool bars, my tongue soured with the taste of iron.

The best the Matron could offer was two Tylenol-plus and a paper cup of water.

"She needs oxycontin," I said.

"Is that what you think?" said the Matron. I could tell she was smirking behind her pink mask. Her hair dyed orange and pulled back in a pony tail, she had the build of an Olympic swimmer.

"It's kidney stones," I said. "We're talking heavy duty pain."

The Matron turned away. "No, sir," she said. "We're not talking at all."

It didn't seem to bother her that the jailer beside her—now wearing one of those cheap blue plastic masks—hadn't covered his nose.

He said, "That means good night." He winked at me, then flicked off the light.

All night I listened to SunMist fight her battle. By the time I saw daylight glowing on the hallway skylight, I was sick with grief. A migraine hammered the back of my eyes.

Knock knock.

Who's there?
Police!
Police who?
Police let me out!

Nonsense like that reverberates through my head when I'm in migraine mode. I'm idiotic with pain. Still, I managed to stand straight when they brought me before the judge. They left SunMist writhing on the floor of her cell. "Indisposed," they told the judge, a silver-haired woman with pink-framed eyeglasses and a small nose. Her forehead was peeling from sunburn. I pictured her fishing all day at the local reservoir.

"You the one with the stolen truck?" she asked.

Her mask was fancy cloth with a big sunflower over it.

Blue Eyes and Sideburns—the troopers—were there, beside me, Blue Eyes with his notebook open, both of them tightly masked.

I raised my voice to make it clear through the mask they'd given me: "As I explained, your honor, that truck was gifted to me by Marty Medeiros in Reno."

"Was Mr. Medeiros with you when you were stopped?"

"No reason for him to be with us. It's not like we're friends."

She studied the charge sheet, then looked up, narrowing her eyes at me: "You don't look well, Mr. Dennis."

"I suffer from migraines," I said. "And epilepsy."

"And your wife?"

"Not my wife," I said. "She wouldn't marry me in a million years. It's kidney stones for her. She's passing one as big as a marble."

Her Honor considered this a moment. "You know as well as I, Mr. Dennis, nobody can pass a stone that big."

I nodded. Then said politely: "I wouldn't tell her that."

Her Honor took hold of her gavel, like she was tempted to make a noise but then thought better of it. She seemed to grimace and said, "We've impounded your truck, confiscated your gun, and euthanized your snake."

"Oh, the poor thing!" I blurted.

"Nothing poor about a rattler," she said.

"He didn't deserve that!" I must've sounded heartbroken. "He did *nothing to nobody*! It was all MY fault."

"Well, there you go," Her Honor said. "That's the key to the whole affair, isn't it—your poor judgment."

I sighed, pulled off my mask to wipe my face.

"Your mask, Mr. Dennis."

I put it back on, those elastic straps biting at the back of my ears. The overhead lights were making my eyes smart. The room seemed to sparkle. At last I said, "With due respect, your honor, what *affair*?"

"Your scheme with the uranium and the illegal liquor."

"That's homemade liquor, nothing illegal about it. Uranium's legal at that weight. I've done nothing wrong."

"Expired license, Mr. Dennis? Unregistered handgun? Stolen truck?"

If they want to get you—because they're bored or desperate or just hard-hearted—they'll get you. Doesn't matter what you might say. And it's not like I had money for a lawyer. Nothing about me gave them pause, much less a scare. To them I was as common and unsavory as roadkill.

We were two days in holding, then the Public Defender

got bail low enough to put us on the street, probably be-cause SunMist's pain was freaking them out. They knew we couldn't run before our court date. Hell, we could hardly walk. I'm not sure where they expected us to stay. Maybe in an alley? Like everywhere else, Winslow has its share of homeless.

The town was so desperate for attractions, it had erected a statue of Jackson Browne on the corner of its main inter-section. Then they built an annual festival around it. That's what you get out here, where nothing much is happening but the heat and dust and a rock-studded horizon.

"You wait here," I told SunMist. Wearing the crummy blue mask they'd given her, she was sitting on a sun-beaten concrete sidewalk bench. I positioned myself to shade her: a big woman with a black rope of hair to her waist. I don't mean ugly big, I mean tall and no-shit strong. Beautiful too. She was in such pain she could hardly talk. There was a blotch of red at her mouth, her lower lip bloodied from biting.

"Wait?" she said at last. "For what?"

"I'm getting us out of here," I said.

"Is that what—" She sucked in a breath. "You want? Prison?"

"You know what we are to them," I said. She leaned for-ward as if to brace herself for a sharp turn. When she re-covered, I continued: "We're *recreation*. A side show. Like freaks at a carnival. That's all."

"We're. Almost. Home."

"Then let's get home," I said.

Zuni land. A sovereign nation. Sure.

I imagined she watched me walk off, maybe watched with affection, even love, because I was taking care of her. Or trying to. It was something I had to prove because nothing else had gone right.

Nobody sets out to be a fuck-up. But every time I came to a turn, it seemed I'd go the wrong way. Let me be clear: my *problem* wasn't about me getting my kicks no matter what. It was about something deep inside me that I couldn't get right, kind of like the needle of a compass that can't find magnetic north.

Didn't take me long to find Winslow's public library. In case you don't know, that's pretty much HQ for the homeless these days: the public library. You got computers, clean bathrooms, and comfy couches. They'll let you stay till closing as long as you don't sleep on the furniture.

I wet my hair down at the water fountain outside, tucked in my T-shirt, tidied my mask. Did I look homeless?

Winslow had no Uber or Lyft, but it did have something called DriveLite. I was able to contact a driver using my Gmail and he got right back to me, said his car was in the shop but he'd borrow a four-wheeler from his neighbor. No worries, he said.

When I returned to SunMist on her bench, he was already there, pulled to the curb in a rusting Blazer. I saw him leaning over the passenger side and talking to her through the open window. Hardly more than a teenager—a still-pimply skinny white kid, probably no more than a wisp of whiskers on his chin. He wore dirty jeans and, despite the heat, a denim jacket over a T-shirt that said, "That's All Folks!" His mask was black, decorated with one of those

Day of the Dead skulls.

SunMist squinted up at me and said, "Fucker's trying to pick me up."

"He's our driver, sweat pea!" Then I leaned into the open window and said, "Hey, man, you couldn't borrow something better than this?" Joking.

The kid seemed to pucker as if to spit. Then: "Nobody forcing you to take a ride with me." He stared with eyes that reminded me of a rabbit.

I helped SunMist into the back. I took the front.

"What's her problem?" the kid asked.

"She'll be okay," I said. "Just get us out of town."

He glanced back at her. "She don't look okay."

Her face was the color of cold oatmeal. But here's the thing: nobody's ever died from passing a kidney stone.

She leaned back and closed her eyes. "Let's get the fuck outta here!"

The kid said his name was Timothy but friends called him Cochise. I couldn't tell if the nickname was ironic, racist, or what.

I said, "You know all about Cochise?"

The kid drove fast. The Blazer shuddered and quaked like it was full of steam and maybe about to explode. Hot wind roared through the open windows.

"Cochise!" the kid nearly shouted over the noise. "Apache warrior from right hereabouts. Fought the Spanish who were trying to settle these parts. Then fought the Americans."

I pulled off my mask. Just too fucking hot.

"You mean the white men," I said.

The kid nodded: "He didn't stand a chance!"

We were already on the interstate, speeding east. It felt good to be moving.

I said, "We're headed for the Zuni reservation."

"You ain't Indian," he said.

"Didn't say I was," I said.

"You married to her?" Like he wanted to be next in line.

"Her name's SunMist," I said. "We might get married." I was able to say this only because I knew she wasn't listening. Saying it made it sound like a wish.

"They didn't kill him," the kid said.

"Cochise?"

"He died on the reservation. Cancer."

"So he's your hero?" I said.

"I wouldn't mind scalping a few people." Then he turned and winked at me. I don't like a child winking at me. It was then I noticed the big Bowie knife in the leather scabbard he had strapped to his right calf.

Men and knives, it's a thing in the West.

At the Holbrook junction, I said, "You want to stay on 40."

The kid didn't seem to hear. He went south on 180.

I said, "You know a better way?"

"Fuck yeah," he said.

I've never had a kid, not that I know of. Couldn't really tell what this one was capable of. A good kid? bad kid? High school drop out? Living in his parents' RV behind their house?

Just then SunMist said, "I've been reading him." She could do that, sometimes know exactly what I was thinking, sometimes read straight through a stranger.

I turned to her: "Who?"

"Him." She pointed. Her eyes were still closed, like she was meditating. "He's gonna rob us."

At first I didn't get it. "What's that, sweet pea?"

The kid glanced at her in the rearview. "She a shaman?"

"She *knows* shamans," I said. Then I got it: this kid wasn't our driver. Just some punk cruising, looking for an opportunity, and here he'd found one. How stupid am I?

I said to him: "Is it true—you're gonna rob us?"

"Yeah, pretty much," he said.

We sped past the south entrance to the Petrified Forest National Park. Tourist season was at its highest. News said everybody was in RVs and tents to get relief from the pandemic. You needed reservations at every campground. I was hoping we'd all get relief in autumn, but some said it'd be years.

I said, "All we want is to get to Zuni land, man. Just go north on 191, then east on 61. It can't be more than fifty miles. I can pay you."

The kid shook his head. "I don't have time for shit like that."

Then, for the longest time, I couldn't bring up a word, never mind I'd always been a talker when trouble came. I was thinking of life before the pandemic, before everybody went mostly crazy. When I met SunMist, I'd been waiting for something good. Like waiting for a bus that was late, that maybe would never come. And then I looked up and there she was. SunMist opened her door and nodded for me come on in and I said to myself, "All right, sir, maybe you are a lucky man after all."

At last I said to the kid, "I got liberty head silver dollars. A whole bag of them."

The kid said, "I never seen silver dollars except in the pawn shop."

He said "the" pawn shop because he knew of only one. That's what we were dealing with.

"You can have them all," I said. "Just get us to Zuni land. It's right on the state line, at the end of 61."

"Told you I can't do that. But for sure I'll take your silver dollars!"

We were coming in to St. Johns, another nowhere town that once had a reason to be but now made you wonder, *Why would anybody...?*

I thought maybe when he slowed for a light, I could jump out. But how was I going to coordinate this with SunMist, who sat in the back holding tight to herself like a woman in labor?

I said, "If you're gonna rob us, maybe you shouldn't be driving. You think of that?"

"Hey, it's no big deal," he said. "I'm not gonna kill you."

"Really?" I said. "That's a relief."

"No way would I do that," he said. "Not somebody like you."

"What's that supposed to mean?"

The kid glanced at me like I was joking. "You don't know, do you?"

"Know what?"

"You're famous, man. *Notorious!*" He handed me his cell phone. "Google 'Arizona Man Driving Stolen Truck.'"

Confused, I held his phone in both hands.

123

"Do it, man!"

I did as he instructed. And there it was: my mug shot and this headline: "Arizona man driving stolen vehicle caught with rattlesnake, uranium, whiskey, and firearm"

I groaned. That photo made me look insane.

SunMist tapped me on the shoulder. "Lemme see."

I passed the phone back to her, then sat there thinking of all the people—like Marty Medeiros—who'd see me online and shake their heads in disgust and mean-spirited glee. *What a loser! What a laugh!*

But it isn't like you think! I wanted to tell them. *It's much more! It's much less!*

"Holy shit," said SunMist. "Why they pickin' on you and not me?"

By this time, we were well out of St. John, speeding north on one of the loneliest highways in the state.

What a laugh! What a loser!

"I need that phone back," the kid said. He held his hand out.

"You want it, you come back here and get it," SunMist said.

"If I come back there," he said, just audible over the wind noise, his voice muffled, "I'm gonna take more than that phone." He extended his open hand farther.

SunMist grabbed his wrist and wrenched it down, hard against the seatback. I heard it snap loud as the crack of a stick. The kid yelped in pain and fright, reared back, letting go of the steering wheel with his left hand. I grabbed the wheel. Now SunMist had him in a choke hold.

"Don't kill him!" I said.

"Little cockroach," she growled, yanking him nearly over the seat. The kid was gargling, his rabbit eyes wide with terror. His right hand flopped useless from his broken wrist. His left hand clawed the headliner for purchase. I was holding the wheel steady. But then he stamped on the accelerator. The engine whined, the Blazer lurched, then the kid kneed the wheel and I lost my grip. We rocketed off the shoulder, rumbling over sage and creosote, their weedy woody scent engulfing us, the Blazer bucking like a shot bronco.

Then—boom!—we stopped nose-busted in a gully, the engine stalled, the smell of gas growing stronger by the second.

"Get out!" I said. "Fast!"

It wasn't easy, the Blazer end-upped about five feet. Sun-Mist and I had to drag out the half-conscious kid. Surprise: the Blazer didn't burst into flames. But it reeked of gas. So all you'd have to do was set a match to it.

That's what I told the kid when he came to: "You wait till sundown," I said. "Then set the thing on fire. You *listening?*"

He was whimpering, his mask gone, his face so red you'd've thought he was having a stroke. He held his useless hand in his lap, like a broken pet.

I butted the sole of his shoe with the toe of my boot: "If you burn it now, we'll make sure they charge you with kidnapping."

He wouldn't look at me.

SunMist said, "It's stolen, I bet."

"Oh, shit." I kneeled in front of the kid and grabbed his free hand. "Is that Blazer stolen?"

The kid gave a feeble shrug with his head, as if to say *maybe*.

I emptied his wallet, took his knife and his phone. I said, "Wait till dark. They'll see the flame for miles."

"Fuck you," the kid said.

I tucked a five into his jacket pocket. "Peace, brother."

We were maybe thirty yards from the road. If you didn't know where to look, you wouldn't have noticed the up-ended Blazer, half hidden by the desert scrub.

A trucker gave us a ride north. SunMist's the one who got his attention. You'd be crazy to ignore a sight like her at the side of the road. It didn't bother him we weren't wearing masks. He had a red MAGA hat on the dash. He said he'd drop us at 61 but then I offered him the confederate bill (with authentication certificate) and a handful of silver dollars. He said he'd take us as far as he could.

"It's my lucky day!" he said. Then he lit a doob and passed it over as if to say, *Fuck Covid!*

I'm not stupid enough to ignore a pandemic but, *Yeah*, I thought, *fuck it*.

By sunset, me and SunMist had stepped over the line into New Mexico's Zuni nation, 723 square miles of it. It'd be just a matter of time before a *grand mal* seizure would take me down, pissed pants and all. But it hadn't taken me down yet. And SunMist seemed to be doing better, walking straight, her mask tucked into her back pocket. "Already, I can feel the power," she said.

DIVERSITY!

Nora and her four fellow Diversity Delegates know they can't say aloud what they're thinking as the noon ferry chugs away from Echo pier on its way to Ebeye, two nautical miles north: *they will smell Ebeye before they see it.* Ebeye is so gross, it's cool to go there, just so you can say you did. Garbage is always smoldering from one end or the other of this little island and, because it's just half the size of American-occupied Kwajalein but has four times the people, it's been called the Calcutta of the Pacific. It's like something from a PBS special. No place is more crowded or trashy. Old, fat, forever sweaty Mister Norman has an explanation for that, like he's got explanations for everything. He's the Advisor to their Diversity Delegates Club. Today he's arranged for them to deliver discarded computers to Ebeye High. It's 2004, a new millennium, and everybody all over the world is online except for the Marshallese!

"You see," Mister Norman explains, "nobody owns land on Ebeye. In fact, all of the islands, every little sand speck of land, are owned by only a handful of families. Most of those families live on Majuro. How far is our capital island from here?" He pauses for an answer and wipes his sunburnt face with a sweat-soaked handkerchief. Until she met Mister Norman, Nora had never seen anyone use a handkerchief except to pretty up the breast pocket of a suit.

Todd Williams answers: "Approximately 300 miles due east." Rumor has it that Todd is still a virgin. Next year he'll be going to Harvard.

Norman nods his satisfaction. "Everybody who isn't a member of those land-owning families—that's about 12,000 Marshallese on Ebeye—all of those people are just renting space. You get what I'm saying? There's no motivation for the Marshallese to build nice houses or plant pretty gardens. As far as they're concerned, they're just passing through."

Nora and Todd and Stef and Tabatha nod like they get it, but they don't get it. If Nora was living here, God forbid, in some sun-blistered tin-roofed shack, she'd do something about it. She'd fix it up. She'd plant flowers, string up some fairy lights, paint her roof blue.

The ferry lurches as the pilot gears down. The ferry is a decommissioned barge-like Army transport with a white tarp strung overtop to keep the sun off. Two new hydrofoil catamarans are being shipped from New Zealand soon to replace these old boats. The world is catching up to the Marshall Islands.

Ferry passengers sit on wooden benches that remind Nora of church pews. The Marshallese women and girls dress in the most colorful muumuus: big bright flowered prints that extend nearly to their ankles. To sit among them is to smell their coconut oil, which they use as hair dressing, perfume, and skin lotion all at once.

Mister Norman paces at the front of the boat, pausing now and then to peer ahead. Nora imagines he's rehearsing his next lecture. The way he talks, you'd think he hated Americans and thought the Marshallese were gods. He married a Marshallese woman who got pregnant by another American twenty years ago when they were all in the Peace Corps. Or so the rumor goes. Rumor also says that his wife stands to make a lot of money if her family can win its suit against the American government for having suffered in the Eniwetok disaster, when the Americans' nuclear fall-out drifted over in 1954 after the big Bikini bomb test. Some say that's why Mister Norman works so hard to make Americans look bad.

He and his wife and their many children live on Majuro, which isn't much better than Ebeye, Nora has heard. Nora has been to Ebeye only once since she's been dating Jeton and that was at Christmas and she and Jeton didn't get a moment alone. Not that there's any place to go on Ebeye. It has no trees to speak of. The "town" is an uneven grid of mostly paved streets; there is shack after shack, only the smallest yards, if any at all, dirt and sand at your feet and overhead a web of electrical wires and phone lines slung from low poles. Stray dogs, cats, and chickens dart past, and stray children, so many children, and idle men, so many idle men, the air smoky from burning garbage or other fire, and Japanese motorbikes speeding by dangerously close.

"In fifty years, all of these islands will be under water," Mister Norman announces, sweeping one hammy, freckled arm towards the small brown mound that is Ebeye in the salt-spray-misty distance.

"Global warming!" Stef blurts, like she's on Jeopardy. *Correction, Ms. Galen: what is Global Warming?*

"Maybe not," Todd Williams says. "If we can reduce our carbon footprint and take measures to build up these islands, we could turn it around. I'm going to work on this in college."

Mister Norman barks a laugh. His yellow teeth remind Nora of ancient ivory she's seen in a museum somewhere and time so deep she can't even imagine how far back it goes, like Mister Norman himself, who looks too old to be teaching, almost too old to be alive.

He snorts: "You do that, Mister Williams, you save us all from oblivion, would you?"

Todd grimaces and kind of shrugs as he leans against the rail and stares at Ebeye. A small funnel of black smoke drifts from one end of the island.

Stef says, almost in protest, "Mister Norman, last week our club, the Environmental Advocates, sold 220 carbon footprint vouchers!"

This makes Mister Norman nearly choke with laughter. He's heaving, his eyes red and tear-filled. "Oh god," he gasps. "Oh, my little hopefuls!" He coughs. He swallows. He sighs: "Oh shit, the world is too much for me!" Then, wiping at his eyes, he sucks up a big breath and says, "Sorry, kids. I know you want to help. And you are helping, aren't you? We've got these computers to deliver, don't we?"

Todd and Stef and Tabatha and Nora sort of nod in agreement but nobody knows what to think. If it's all a joke, if the world is already ruined the way Mister Norman says it is, then what's the point?

Bringing gifts to Ebeye makes Nora feel good—like she's putting herself on the line somehow. Most Americans wouldn't dare come here, even though it's only two miles away. The Marshallese people, really, are very nice, even if they don't have a fraction of the cool stuff Americans have.

"We go for the wrong reasons," Mister Norman says, still wiping at his eyes, "and we do the wrong things, but it's better than not going at all."

He's hilarious when he talks like that, Nora has decided. He's as close to a crazy person as she will ever meet.

Here's the coolest thing about the trip: Nora's parents have no idea she's on Ebeye. They can't keep up with her many co-curricular activities. She's planning to surprise Jeton, who hasn't been able to get near her since she got grounded after her parents caught them fucking on the patio last week.

God, did that freak them out!

As soon as the DDs step off the boat, Todd and Stef wheeling the computers on a freight dolly, a crowd of children swarm after them.

Mister Norman has taught the DDs how to say the official greeting: "Io̧kwe!" Which sounds like "Yuck-way!"

"Don't you surrender a penny!" he warns—because the children are always asking for money. Even a quarter is a big deal to them.

He calls the Republic of the Marshall Islands "a nation of children" because the average age of its citizens is, like, sixteen: a fact that makes Nora giddy with fantasies about how different the world would be if the teens ruled! There's nothing teens couldn't do, if only the grown-ups would let them.

"Sup?" the little kids are saying. Most don't have shirts; none have shoes; and a couple of the smallest don't even have undies. Playing in puddles, dragging sticks and palm fronds behind them, chasing dogs, they look happy enough. And nobody appears hungry.

"Who looks after the children?" Nora asks.

"Their parents are working or looking for work or fishing," Mister Norman says. "There's probably a cousin or aunt nearby."

The causeway construction is the biggest employer now. It will connect Ebeye to the several islands just north of it, which will create more room for all of these people. Mister Norman says that space is so precious out here in the Marshalls a California company has been trying to get the Republic to build landfill with American garbage. "If that's not the most fucked-up proposal you've ever heard, I don't know what is," he said. "But, hell, why not? We've already dumped all kinds of atomic fallout on these people, haven't we?"

He went off on that one for about an hour. Nora calls his rants "the Norman Invasion."

Mister Norman is leading the way, right down the middle of the street, which has been paved recently. The shacks on either side are painted as varied and brightly colored as the women's muumuus. And every fifth house seems to be a small church.

Mister Norman walks so fast, Todd and Stef can't keep up, pushing that heavy cart.

"Mister Norman, slow down," Nora calls.

He stops. Then a motorcyclist speeds by, nearly swiping him.

"Eājāj wōt!" he shouts after it.

Nora assumes this is a curse, though it could mean anything, like "thanks a lot!"

"Sup? Got a quarter?" a little boy asks Nora.

She shrugs in response.

"Quarter?" he repeats.

Then Mister Norman shoos him away.

Suddenly the sky opens up, a pile of afternoon thunderheads having tumbled in. Nora and her companions are drenched within a minute. Leaving the cart of computers at the curb, they seek shelter under the corrugated tin overhang of the Independent Baptist Church, which at a glance looks like another shack.

"See that?" Mister Norman says, nodding like the know-it-all he is. "That's why I had you secure the computers under a plastic tarp."

Then, like a message from God, a Toyota pickup roars down the street in the torrent and slams full into the cart, computer parts spilling and spinning like shrapnel—and making such a loud smack! that Nora, Stef, and Tabatha scream in unison.

The truck screeches to a stop, sliding several yards, the rain still gushing like whitewater.

"Serves us right," Mister Norman says in disgust, stepping into the torrent. "Serves us fucking right!"

The driver clambers out. "Very sorry," he says. He looks Indian and he's young, of course, but not a teenager. Like most Marshallese men, he's wearing khaki trousers and a t-shirt. The Marshallese love American t-shirts! This one says "AC/DC" across the front.

Then the rain stops—just like that—and the sun comes out, rays glinting from the blue-oily puddles on the asphalt, and the children are playing again, dogs barking after them, and the air is smoky again with the smell of burning garbage and maybe barbecued pig.

The driver helps Mister Norman and the DDs pick up the wrecked computers, but many of the pieces disappear with the children, who dart in and out, grabbing what they can as if this were a game. The DDs load the junk into the back of the man's pickup, then the man drives Mister Norman and the DDs to the high school. But no one at the high school seems to know that the computers were coming. A stout middle-aged Marshallese woman nods "yes' to everything Mister Norman says but she can't tell him anything he wants to know.

It's so un-PC to say it, but all middle-aged Marshallese women look alike to Nora. They are short and stocky and have thick black and/or graying hair that's been cut to the shoulders or tied back in a knot. And they wear long flowered dresses and no make-up and still have nice smiles but every last one of them seems to have let herself go. It must be all the children they've had. You can't keep up with all those children. Nora has promised herself that she'll have only one child. Well, maybe two. Or maybe none. But she won't ever let herself go.

She and Stef and Todd and Tabatha help the driver unload the broken computers onto the sidewalk. The sun is so hot, they are almost dry from the downpour already. Nora feels a trickle of sweat skid across her spine. She'd like to be fresh for Jeton but it looks like it's not going to happen. She thought there'd be a ceremony or some gathering where she'd see him. He doesn't even know she's here! She can forget trying to find his house because there are no street numbers, no directories, no maps that will show her where he lives. And Jeton doesn't own a cell phone.

"You're wasting your money," Jeton tells his cousin Mike.

Mike is on the video machine, playing Space Spiders. He says, "I got money to waste."

The machine goes Ka-blam! ka-blam! ka-blam! as Mike muscles into it.

Jeton slugs down half the Tsingtoa Mike has just bought him, letting the foam burn his throat.

They are at the Lucky Star Bar and Restaurant, where Jeton hopes Mike will buy him a lunch of shrimp lo mein. The Lucky Star is dark, like all the drinking places, with only a single plastic window up front and a few light bulbs strung over the bar, which is a painted countertop made of chipboard from the Philippines. A few young men Jeton doesn't know sit at a table near the window; they are laughing and seem to have money. Maybe they are from Majuro. Two old men sit at the end of the bar watching the TV, which sits on a box behind the counter. The program—something in Spanish—comes by satellite from Manila.

Jeton should be in school and Mike should be at the causeway but "Fuck it," Jeton said when Mike met him this morning. Mike told him that they would take the "day off," as the Americans put it.

Mike is two years older than Jeton and much lighter-skinned—wūdmouj—because one of his grandfathers was Japanese. Mike also has a fine black mustache that Jeton admires. And, unlike Jeton, who is short and has thick legs, Mike is tall and has an easy stride. Jeton thinks sometimes that Mike is the man he should be. But it is becoming clear to Jeton that he will not be like Mike, who has a high school diploma and has traveled as far as Japan and now drives a loader for the construction crew on the Causeway.

Mike's plan is to sell electronics on Ebeye, ship them direct from China, he says, and make a "fuckin' fortune."

Jeton's plan is—or was—to love Nora forever. Since their trouble with her parents last week and Nora's surprising announcement about returning to the States, Jeton has felt jebwābwe, like doing something crazy. Nora's parents may ask the American police to ban Jeton from returning to Kwajalein. Americans can do that to the ri-Majeḷ because the Americans have paid the Republic a lot of money to build their missiles on the island.

In seven days Nora flies away.

Jeton met her for the first time when his high school soccer team played the American high school soccer team. Jeton was the ri-Majeḷ goalie. Already he had lost one tooth up front from protecting the goal. Nora said the missing tooth made his smile look "cute."

"You hungry?" he asks Mike.

Ka-blam! Mike is already at level twelve, alien spiders raining from the video sky: ka-blam! ka-blam! ka-blam! blam!blam!blam! So much noise, Mike's handsome eyes expertly scanning the screen, his thumbs pummeling the joysticks.

"Sounds like one of us is hungry," Mike says at last.

Jeton wants Mike's money but, at the same time, he doesn't want to see Mike spend so much. If Mike keeps spending what he makes, he will never open his electronics shop. This is a frustrating thought because it is so American, worrying about what has not happened yet. Jeton suspects this comes from spending time with Nora.

He says, "Mike, what happened to your electronics business?"

"I'm saving for it right now," Mike answers.

"Right *now*?"

"Fuck you, Jeton. Least I got a job."

Ka-blam! Level 15. The game is over. Without glancing at Jeton, Mike feeds the machine more dollars and starts again.

Jeton looks with envy at the custom chopsticks Mike carries in a leather case from a loop at his belt. The chopsticks, carved from whale bone, he got from his Japanese grandfather before the old man died.

"Let me try," Jeton says.

Mike glances at him and smiles. "You don't got the reflexes."

Jeton sputters his indignation. "Best goalie on Ebeye—I got reflexes!"

Mike lets him have his seat. The blue-green alien spiders drift down from the yellow video sky like ash Jeton has seen raining over the Ebeye landfill. When the pretty spiders touch Jeton's fat little space ships, the ships explode.

"You got to blow them up," Mike instructs. "Fire, man!"

Jeton thumbs the joysticks, jerking them as he fires with both barrels. Ka-blam! ka-blam! ka-blam! so loud it hurts his ears, spiders splintering into shards like glass against rock, rockets streaking red lines across the screen, more and more spiders falling, his ships exploding until Jeton pushes himself away from the machine in frustration.

"Fuck it!" he says, his face burning. He wants to slam the video screen with his fist.

"You don't have to get angry, man. It's a game."

"Fuck it. I never liked these bwebwe machines."

"You're like a old man, Jeton. These machines gonna make me a million dollars."

"You don't got enough to buy a machine like this."

Mike sits again at his machine, then feeds it more dollars. "Not today."

"When?" There it is, Jeton thinks. They are talking like the ri-pālle. "Tomorrow? Next week? Next year?"

"What do you care, Jeton?"

Ka-blam! Mike starts firing. He is steady, relentless, his eyes focused. Maybe he can do what he says. Maybe Jeton needs to be like Mike when he plays video. See the alien spiders and shoot, see them and shoot. Shoot shoot shoot. No letting up.

"I *don't* care," Jeton lies. "I'm gonna—"

His sudden assertion stops him because he is not sure what he is going to do or be. It seems everyone else has a plan.

"You gonna?" Mike goads.

"I'm gonna be goalie on the national team."

The national soccer team trains on Majuro. They fly to Manila, Tokyo, and Sidney to play other teams. The star goalie, Abbetar, wears no shoes and has lost five of his front teeth saving the ball. Who could be tougher than Abbetar?

Mike laughs once. "You replace Abbetar?"

What is it the Americans say? "Stranger things have happened."

"You come over to the causeway," Mike says, still firing, alien spiders splintered into purple bits. "Maybe I can get you work."

"The causeway is a mistake," Jeton says. He watches Mike's face to see what happens. "I heard all about it when I was on Kwajalein."

"What you hear?" Mike is up to level 10 already.

"It's gonna ruin the lagoon because it blocks the waves."

Ka-blam! "Nothing can ruin the lagoon," Mike says. Ka-blam!

Jeton finishes his beer. "It blocks the waves."

"It doesn't block the waves. I work on it. I see."

"Ibwijleplep. Storm waves. The American engineers say so."

"They say that because they aren't building it."

"We ri-Ṃajeḷ don't know how to build anything," Jeton says. "We're stupid."

"*I'm* not stupid," Mike says. "And I'm building the fuck-ing causeway."

That's better, Jeton thinks. He's got Mike mad.

"Causeway's gonna ruin everything," Jeton continues. "You should quit."

The spiders are coming so fast, Mike can't stop them. Suddenly he loses the game, his ships disappearing in a black and blue video cloud.

"Fuck you," Mike says. "Fuck you!"

Jeton isn't sure if he's saying this to the machine or to him.

"Good reflexes," Jeton mocks.

Mike stands up slowly, wipes his hands on his blue jeans, then—without looking at Jeton—turns away and walks to the door. He has the kind of intent, closed-up look on his face that Jeton has seen on men who fight cocks.

"Your causeway ruins us!" Jeton calls after him.

As soon as Mike is gone and the door has shut out the bright sunlight again, Jeton feels terrible. Why has he treat-ed his cousin so badly?

He hears the young men laughing from the front of the room. Maybe laughing at him. He hears the Spanish pro-gram speaking its trilling language from the TV set behind the bar. And somewhere at the back of his mind he hears the video game blowing up spiders and spaceships. None of it is worth hearing. None of it makes sense.

When he gets outside, to the rain-puddled street, the air thick with lunch-time aromas—of bwiin-enno, fried leeks and sausage—he does not see Mike. Small children who should be in school are playing tag, darting from and through the narrow paths between the hunched-up houses. Like shrimp in tide pools, Jeton thinks. Several young men and a few older men are sitting in the shade of a breadfruit tree nearby, sharing cigarettes. Men and women are walking away from him, each carrying a straw or plastic bag, on their way to catch the two o'clock ferry to Kwajalein.

Jeton knows that when he sees Mike again, Mike will have forgotten that Jeton was so kajjōjō, hateful. That is how it is with the ri-Majel. Americans are different: they will not let you forget anything.

Jeton could jaba, hang-out, with the men by the tree but they are going to talk about women and Jeton doesn't want to talk about his.

Maybe he will go to the pier, where there are a couple of bars and restaurants. Maybe someone will offer to buy him a bowl of fried egg and rice.

He could go home, but no one is there. His mother is a maid on Kwajalein, his sister a checker at the Americans' supermarket there. His younger brother and sister are at school. Or maybe playing in the alleys. His older brother is on Majuro working with his father, who makes soap in the copra factory. They visit Ebeye every three months, bringing with them samples from the factory and smelling of coconut that seems to have gotten into their breath and become a part of their body sweat.

This is something else he never thought of until he met Nora. His smell. Nora says to him, "I love your smell. It's so *un-American.*" This seems to be a good thing, though Jeton doesn't know what it means. And he is afraid to ask. Where is Nora now? He wants to fuck her bad. He wants to love her hard. He wants to be with her forever.

"These are the only places you'll find authentic Marshallese food," Mister Norman announces. He's treating the DDs to lunch at one of Ebeye's "take-out" shops, a plywood shack, about five by four feet, with a single large open window for service. "We should try some jukjuk, coconut-rice balls, and bwiro, preserved breadfruit."

The woman inside looks to Nora like every middle-aged Marshallese woman she's seen: heavy, her hair pulled back but messy from the humidity, her face broad and friendly and without a dab of makeup. She wears a cotton shift of a brightly flowered pattern.

Her take-out is well-provisioned, the shelves behind her displaying stacks of Huggies disposable diapers, cans of Starkist tuna, boxes of Kellogg's Frosted Flakes, piles of Snickers candy bars, and stacked tins of SPAM, the national favorite. None of it cheap.

Mister Norman pays for the "real food," as he calls it, then passes it around.

Tabatha grimaces at the brownish paste on her pandanus leaf. "Is this gonna make us sick?"

"It's a miracle the crap you eat every day doesn't make you sick," Mister Norman answers, downing a handful of raw papaya strips—which are so crunchy they sound like potato chips as he chews.

Nora pretends to enjoy the Diversity lunch but all she can think about is finding Jeton and walking with him on the beach. They have so little time left together! Before Gus and Jan grounded her, they let Nora meet Jeton one more time—in the neutral zone of Kwajalein's Emon beach on a Saturday afternoon. Jeton showed up looking sweaty and worried, his visitor's tag clipped to the tail of his t-shirt. Nora was sitting on a picnic table in the only empty pavilion. She patted the plastic bench for him to sit beside her. Nervously, he glanced beyond the pavilion, then pecked her on the forehead. It was the usual blinding sunny afternoon, big silver-white clouds floating fast in a dreamy blue sky. Children were frolicking noisily in the swim area, marked off with orange floats. Some teenagers were water skiing farther out, several of them sprawled on the ski deck. Though Nora knows she could do it if she tried—she's an athlete—she hasn't learned to water ski in the two years she's been living on Kwaj. Ironic, isn't it? Like living in Manhattan and never visiting the Statue of Liberty. It's something she'll joke about with her college friends, she has decided.

The secret truth is, she's afraid to swim out to the ski deck. It's moored over the drop-off, where the white sand falls away hundreds of feet into the black-blue depths of the lagoon. *The drop-off!* You're swimming along in the bath-warm water and you can see the squiggly white-sandy coral-studded bottom and then suddenly it's gone and the water goes cold as a deep-bottom current surrounds you and there's nothing below but darkness, not a single fish anymore, and it's like you're all alone in the world—you might as well be in the middle of the ocean. A shark or *something* could snatch you in an instant and drag you down and nobody would be able to help you. *Gone!* That's what the drop-off is about. That's why Nora has never learned to ski.

When Nora told Jeton she got accepted to Sacramento State and would be living with her grandparents next year, Jeton fell silent and drew back. He kept turning his head and squinting at her like she'd suddenly gone invisible.

"College!" she exclaimed. "Aren't you happy for me?"

After a long silence, Jeton staring at the sandy concrete below his feet, he said, "You could go to college here."

"Majuro?" she answered. "That's *junior* college, Jeton. Sacramento State is a *real* college, the whole four years."

He wiped at his face and pushed back his pretty black hair. "When does this college start?"

"September," she said. "But I'm flying to Sacramento right after graduation."

"June?"

"Jan and Gus insist," she explained sadly.

"Because we are fucking?"

"Yeah, I guess."

"You told them you love me?"

She sighed. In some ways Jeton is just a boy. How could she explain that there is love and then there is *love*? Sure, she loves him. She's never loved anybody more! But what does that mean, really? If she had to tell him the truth, she'd admit that all of this out here, as nice as it is, with the free movies and the year-round summer and all the great kids to hang with, it's like a dream. None of it *sticks*—that's what she'd like to explain to Jeton. What really matters is life in the States, where people take notice. Most people in the States don't even know about Kwajalein, this little piece of America in the middle of the Pacific Ocean!

"You're happy for me, right?" Nora asked again.

Jeton, her lover, her sweet, good man, nodded yes. "You're the best," he said.

That nearly brought tears to her eyes. She kissed him on the mouth. She didn't care who was watching. Then she kissed him again. Then he pulled away and said, kind of breathlessly, "I gotta go."

"I'm way grounded," she reminded him.

"They can't keep us apart," he said. Then he took on his goalie look, like he was about to meet the opposing team.

"Let me see what I can do," she said—to calm him down because she knew he might do something crazy, the way he's crazy on the soccer field. Like he doesn't care what happens to himself.

"You can come to Ebeye?" He sounded surprised.

"I can come," she promised.

And here she is. She's not big-headed or anything but sometimes, really, she thinks she's super blessed. It's not like she's especially good or holy or anything like that. But sometimes the greatest things happen to her. Like she's standing here, eating this Marshallese paste with her Diversity Delegates and Mister Norman is luging on one of his bobsled rants about nuclear fallout, how America tested H-bombs in the Marshalls *forever*—sixty seven bombings in all—and the fallout was horrible and the Marshallese got all fucked up and deformed and the money the Americans gave hardly covered the cost of relocating people to different islands and nobody but nobody can clean up the places that were bombed, it's gonna take, like, a million years. . . . So

Mister Norman is going on the way he does—one of his "invasions"—and then, out of nowhere, Jeton walks up to her and says, "Hi, lijera."

And Nora nearly fucking faints!

It's a Hollywood moment that the senior class is going to be talking about for weeks!

So Nora takes Jeton in her arms and plants a big one on his gorgeous lips. And now Jeton looks like he's about to faint because, as Mister Norman will tell you, the Marshallese just don't do PDAs!

Then, as if announcing she's going down the hall for a drink of water, Nora says she and Jeton are going to take a little walk.

"That's fine," Mister Norman says. "We'll be right behind you."

Nora and Jeton walk on the oceanside, the best place Jeton can think to take her because everywhere else is too crowded. He once told her that Ebeye is the most wonderful place on earth. He described the sweet scent of fried onions, the smoky aroma of grilled chicken, the muddy alleys, the crowds of giddy children, the bright blues, reds, yellows, and greens of painted plywood, the laundry flagging on lines behind every home, the sputter and stink of motorbikes, the chaos of radio music, the yelping of dogs. . . . But now, with her at last on his island, he is sure that she cannot appreciate these things.

There is too much garbage, he realizes—disposable diapers washed up like dead fish and plastic Coke bottles and bright white chunks of Styrofoam from broken beer coolers. This is why Americans think the Marshallese are dirty. Just beyond the garbage-strewn sand, four small children are afloat in a doorless refrigerator. Flagging their arms, they shout in triumph as shallow waves push their boat to the shore a few feet, then suck it out a few feet, back and forth. The tide is coming in, the reef exposed in high places, sun glinting from trapped water.

Carefully, Jeton says, "The best islands are to the east in the Ralik chain. Everybody says so."

"Really?" Nora says, though he can tell she is only being polite.

"There is one called Wotje. The Japanese brought dirt from Japan to make a grand garden there."

"You mean during World War II?"

"Yes, long ago." Gingerly he toes aside a disposable diaper. "It is very beautiful."

"Are you going to move there?" she asks.

"With you," he says, wanting this to sound like a promise or a proposal. But it sounds so much like a question he secretly berates himself: bōkāro!

"I told you I have to go to college, Jeton."

"Nobody is *making* you go, Nora."

"I want to!"

When he doesn't answer, she adds: "You could go too."

"I am no good in school."

"You could start with junior college—on Majuro."

It tires him to hear her talk like this, pretending that he is as smart as she. "Why do you say these things you know are not possible?"

"Because I believe in you!" she says. "Because anything's possible, isn't it?"

"Anything?" he says. He wants to tell her that this is a lie. Is it possible to make Nora stay? Is it possible to make her realize that he cannot follow her? that he will never be like her?

Americans like to argue. Since being with Nora, he has learned this. It irritates him, and scares him, that he is drawn to arguments that get him nowhere. He has promised himself that he will not be a baby—eokkwikwi—who cries for her attention or a baka fool who believes she will do whatever he wants just because he says she should. After so many arguments with Nora, he understands for the first time what she has meant by the expression "get real." Money is real to Nora. Plans are real to Nora. The future is real to Nora. So he will give her all of that by letting her believe that he agrees with everything she says. It is the curse of the ri-Ma-jeļ to be so giving, so polite. It is why they call "love to you" when they meet a stranger, even one who will destroy them.

It feels like they're having an argument, but it isn't an argument. Jeton is being too polite. He's calling her lijera but not bati—"pretty one" but not "lover." He's saying "yes" a lot. It's what the Marshallese do when they're shut down. They get super agreeable. It can be irritating, the way it's beginning to irritate Nora now. "I'll see you at the game tomorrow," she reminds him.

"Yes," he says. It could be "yes" to anything. It's going to rain tomorrow. *Yes.* It's too fucking hot here all the time. *Yes.*

She says, "Don't be sad, Jeton. We've got a little time."

"Yes." He won't even look at her.

"Whatever," she sighs.

"Let's go," Mister Norman commands, pushing his way through the dockside crowd.

As it turned out, they left their broken computers on the curb in front of the high school. There was no ceremony. But the woman at the high school thanked them anyway.

"At least we tried," Tabatha says.

Jeton doesn't kiss Nora at the dock. He wouldn't in front of all these people who know him. But it's not embarrassment, it's something else, like pride and modesty and a warped kind of protectiveness Nora has never been able to figure out. Suddenly she's really down. The day hasn't turned out anything like she wanted.

As the ferry chugs away from the Ebeye dock, the air fusty with diesel exhaust and the stink of dead coral, the world seems too painfully beautiful to Nora. Behind the big cotton-ball clouds on the horizon, the sky is lit up with huge fingers of orange, yellow, and fuchsia. On the pier-end, Jeton stands among a crowd of small children, everybody waving except him. Nora feels the firm hand of grief tighten around her throat. Maybe he won't show for the game tomorrow and she'll never see Jeton deGroen, her handsome young man, again! She thinks of his fearless saves at the soccer goal, how proud he is to have lost a tooth from playing hard. He would save her just as ardently, she decides, if she would let him.

The many small children around him continue waving frantically, even though they can't possibly know anyone on the ferry back to Kwajalein. Everybody on the boat is ri-pālle: ri, meaning people; pālle meaning pale. It sounds like "ree-belly." The *pale people*. It is one of many words Nora has learned from Jeton.

Then, like the distant rumble of thunder on a cloudless day, she hears Mister Norman behind her saying: "You broke his heart, didn't you?"

Puzzled, she turns to him. She can't tell whether his look is one of disgust or dismay. Or pity?

"I don't know what you're talking about," she lies.

"Don't you?" he says.

She wants to answer yes, of course, she knows what she's done—she fell in love and loved as hard as she could, Jeton never doubting that she was his and he was hers, but now it's over because she's growing up, she has college to attend and a life to make, she can't stop now, she certainly can't stop here in the middle of the ocean just because she's had an affair with a beautiful boy. Jeton understands this, that's why he's smiling, wishing her the best, because he knows that he's got a future too, that she's not limiting him, that the Compact of Free Association allows him to travel to the States, where he can attend college and make his own way however he wants, and who knows? she and he could meet again, anything could happen, and if that *did* happen wouldn't it be proof finally that they were meant for each other?

But this brief romance during their senior year, this isn't proof of anything, it's just a sweet interlude before better things and Jeton knows this like she knows this, *so back off, Mister Norman, you sour old fuck, why are you so intent on making everybody miserable with your negativity?*

Within an instant, Nora is ready to say all of this evenly and intently to the old man, who's looking at her as if she were the most pathetic girl. *You are so ignorant!* she wants to snap. But instead, to her surprise and sudden shame, she finds herself bawling into Tabatha Duggin's shoulder, stunned to think that maybe she doesn't know who she is or what she's doing.

WHEELS

1: DONNER PASS

There's no easy way to get out of Nevada. Either you scratch through the badlands or climb over the mountains. My way was mountains. There was snow in the pass. Highway Patrol wouldn't let me by without chains or four-wheel drive. On the shoulder, three coveralled men were ready to rent me chains for fifty plus a deposit. As I slowed, they went at my wagon like a NASCAR crew. The cute one with the wind-burned face and sun-bleached soul patch, tapped at my window. I rolled down. He said: "Cash or Visa only, doll."

I gave him cash. His fingers were brown from rust. I heard the chains knuckling at my wheelwell. Someone said, "Jesus shit!"

Soul patch said, "You need a receipt?"

"For my deposit," I reminded him.

He nodded and almost smiled, still counting ones. My tip jar take.

Snow fell like confetti, the sky the color of stainless steel.

My mother had said on the phone: *He just kneeled down, Rainy. Like he was about to pray.*

They'd been working the line, grading oranges, she said, and Dad's collapse was nothing more than that: a sudden kneel. She worked across from him. Everybody thought this romantic. Until a few months ago he'd been a foreman in the groves. After his third faint, they put him on the line.

It pissed me off, how he and Mom had let it go on without checking.

Soul-patch handed me a damp slip of paper. Rusted fingerprints. He smiled. I wanted to lick his chapped lips.

"You do this all day?" I asked.

He renewed his smile: "You gonna tell me to quit?"

"I wouldn't do that," I said.

I thought of my live-in, Kai. He wanted me to quit gigging: *Nobody does the road like that anymore, Rain. It's cliché.*

I'd wanted him to say: *You're too good, babe, you deserve more.*

The cliché was how we related. Whenever I needed him to be better than me, I could predict every wrong thing he'd say.

Soul-patch said, "Think about it. I'm saving lives, you know."

I thought I heard him say, *You don't have to drive through snow.*

So I said, "I don't?"

He raised his snowy eyebrows at me.

Then I heard at last what he'd said and I felt my face grow hot.

I was twelve when we visited Donner Pass on our way to a week in Reno. The Donner family ate everything they could—harnesses, shoes, tree bark—before they started eating each other. As I lay by the motel pool that week while my parents played the slots and my brother watched cable, I thought of the Donners, and asked myself: *Would you have done any better?*

Soul-patch cleared his throat. I'd been staring.

"Sorry," I said.

He seemed to shrug without shrugging.

Then I raised the window. Someone thumped my trunk. I got a final chain-fit, then rolled away, clanking. Glancing in my rearview, I saw nobody waving.

2: EXETER, CA

"He's sleeping," Mom said. "Don't make a sound."

She pecked me on the forehead. The screen door creaked as I edged past. Her porch was crowded with plants, plastic tacked over the screens. I wanted to explain why I was parked on the front lawn. She smelled of cinnamon and something else. Maybe beer.

"I'm not asleep," Dad called.

He was lying in his recliner, the TV murmuring a few feet away.

I said, "You scared me, Dad."

"Serves you right."

He was smiling—or trying to. The left side of his face was frozen.

"Don't get up," I said.

"I'm not."

I tried to kiss his cheek but he squirmed and I got his ear instead.

He was wearing white wool socks, corduroy pants that were worn at the knees, and a gray sweatshirt that said in pink script, *Get it now while it's hot!*

"You must be exhausted," Mom said to me. "How long'd it take?"

"Not that long," I lied.

"I saw there was snow in the pass." Dad gestured to the TV. He was watching the weather channel.

"It's February, Dad."

"Smarty pants." He tried another smile.

I realized I might not get used to the way his face looked. It was like staring at a cracked mirror.

"I'm about to make some pork chops," Mom announced. "You want one or two?"

I turned to see if she was joking. I'd been a vegetarian since high school.

Mom was looking at me—enthused and hopeful—like I was her younger sister. A few years ago this would have infuriated me.

"Sweetheart, she wants a salad."

"We've got salad in a bag," she offered. "And five kinds of dressing."

"Thanks." I sat on the battered ottoman next to Dad's recliner. "So, what's the latest?"

He turned down the TV with the remote. "Your mom's learning to cook."

Dad did all the cooking when we were growing up. Mom washed the dishes. He cleaned the bathroom. She did the laundry. That was their deal.

"I'm not supposed to move," he added.

Mom leaned away from the stove to show herself in the kitchen doorway. "He moves plenty."

I heard the sizzling of meat. A moment later I smelled it.

Dad said, "You were gigging in Elko or was it Winnemucca?"

"You need to give us your latest CD," Mom said. Smoke poured from her pan.

"It's just a club band," I said.

"You don't have a CD?"

"No."

"Well, what do you play every night?" Dad asked.

"Old covers."

"You like that?" he said.

"It's a job."

Squinting through the smoke, Mom stabbed at the meat with a long fork. "Are you going to change jobs?"

"Drumming's a hard business," Dad said solemnly.

"Every job is hard business," I said.

"You can always drum on the side."

I looked at them, back and forth, as if to say, *How many times have we been through this?*

Then the smoke alarm went off.

3: FROZEN ORANGES

"You quit your gig and go home and this is the first I hear?" Kai was complaining.

"I can go back if I want."

"But you don't want, right?"

I was in my parents' front yard, my cell to my ear. It was nine or ten and frosty already. Inside, Dad was sleeping on his recliner, the TV on. Mom was sitting on the couch nearby, afraid to wake him. Or watching to see that he was still breathing.

"It's cold here," I said.

"Leaving is quitting," he said.

"Are you *scolding* me?"

I heard him sigh. Then: "How are we gonna pay the bills?"

"Tell me you're joking," I said. "Please."

"One of us has to be practical."

"You've been begging me to quit for years."

"How many years?" he said. "We've been together for only three."

"Seems like longer," I said. When he didn't answer, I said. "I couldn't stay out there anymore. You don't know what it's like."

"Sure, I do. You tell me all the time."

"Motels feel like tombs," I said. "And the desert—"

"Didn't you, like, *grow up* in a desert?"

"The San Joaquin isn't exactly a desert."

"You've got rattlesnakes and road runners and tarantulas in the Valley. That's not a desert?"

"It's where I grew up."

"So what are you telling me, you're going to live with your parents?"

"I couldn't do that even if I wanted to," I said.

I'd introduced Kai to my parents only a year ago, at my brother's wedding. What did that say?

"I'm confused, Rainy. What the fuck do you want?"

"I hate it here." Phone to my ear, I walked to the middle of the street. Exeter has the widest streets of any small town I've seen. There's no explanation for it.

This was a neighborhood of shotgun shacks and bungalows, most built for workers between 1920 and 1940. Modest folk like my parents. Nothing here was made to last.

I said, "I love it here too."

"Kind of the way you feel about me, is that it?"

"Yeah, that's right."

"I love you too," he said. "Come home and we'll argue for real. Maybe you'll lock me out of the apartment again and I can spend the night in your van, using a cymbal for a pillow."

"You won't ever let me forget that, will you?"

"It's love, Rainy. It's all good."

"I haven't heard from you *in a week*, Kai!"

"Not true. I texted a few days ago."

"Oh, yeah: 'working on a new recipe'—isn't that what you wrote?"

"I thought you'd want to know."

"The least you can do is give me an update on Harriet." My Basset Hound.

"Right, I could have done that."

"She's okay?"

"Of course. You miss her more than you miss me, *n'est-ce pa?*"

"Don't force me to pick a favorite," I said. "What have you been doing besides cooking new recipes?"

"Selling your CDs on Telegraph Avenue."

"For real?"

"It's pocket change but it keeps me afloat."

"Don't be cruel, Kai."

He howled, imitating Harriet.

I slapped my phone shut.

In the distance I heard the turbines start up. They'd churn the air all night to keep the freeze off the oranges. Valencias this time of year. In the old days, hands had to go into the fields to light the smudge pots. When small, I used to sing those words to myself: *smudge pots smudge pots smudge pots smudge pots!*

My cell chirped. It was 2007 and I was the only musician I knew who didn't have a music download on her phone.

"I'm an asshole," Kai said.

Behind him the TV blared.

I said, "You know my Dad nearly died?"

"Nobody told me anything!" he said, as if I were blaming him. Then: "Shit, Rain. How is he?"

"Half his face is frozen. It's weird."

"How long you gonna stay?"

"I don't know."

"You got money?"

"Do you?"

His program director had given him a six-month extension to finish his dissertation, which was a year overdue. I admitted to myself that it'd bug me if Kai didn't finish.

I said, "I got enough to hold me a month."

"So you're getting out of the music biz?" He could have

been talking about the weather.

"You got suggestions?"

"I would *never.*"

"Smart man."

Then we were silent.

Kai said: "You know I'm fucked up when you're not here."

I listened to the TV behind him and, behind me, the props motoring above the orchards. "Then you must be fucked up a lot."

"Isn't that what I've been saying?"

This was the best he could do. Why did I want more?

"I'll call you," he promised.

"I know you will," I said.

4: BLOODY CUTICLES

Mom was still up when I came in.

"What are you going to do?" she asked.

"Me?" I said. *"What about you?"*

"You know what I do."

"Ignore the painful truth?" I regretted my words immediately.

She didn't blink. "What would the truth be, Rainy?"

That you're dreaming if you think Dad's going back to work. That from now on, your life is going to be harder than you've ever imagined. That I don't make enough money to help you and I can't bring myself to move back to Exeter—and I feel like a fuck-up for it.

I sighed. "I probably shouldn't have quit the band."

She played along: "You can go back."

"I could."

"Is this an integrity thing?"

A few years back I'd explained to her the difference between an "integrity band" and a "factory band." The first plays music that matters. The second plays music that pays.

"Integrity or not," I said, "musicians like me are a dying breed."

"That's why you love it. You've always driven against the traffic."

"That sounds like an insult," I said.

"You wanted to talk about truth."

"So I should go to college, get a degree, and join the hive—like my big brother?"

"Mark is happy."

"Mark is miserable."

"He just got married, Rainy!"

"He's *gay*, Mom!"

"You don't know that."

"I feel for him, I really do. If only he'd come out."

"He's the *manager* of a *division*!"

"He'd rather be managing a greeting card shop in the Castro. You just wait."

"The Castro?"

"In the City."

"What city?"

"San Francisco. What other city could there be?"

"Sacramento. Fresno. Visalia. Modesto?"

"Now you're depressing me."

"You take such pride in turning your back on the place you're from," she said sadly. "You *loved* it here when you were a girl!"

We'd race our bikes through the dirt tracks of the groves, wheeling over fallen oranges, their rot a sweet punky smell. In spring, their white blossoms would rain over us like lumped flakes of tumbling snow. Concrete irrigation ditches, ten-foot-deep, would flood with green-black water, sluice-fast and roiled with eddies. We'd toss in our flip flops to watch them twirl madly and float away.

After high school, I couldn't get away fast enough.

"I'm not a girl." Suddenly I was very tired.

"You're all of twenty-nine," she said sadly. "And trying so hard to grow up."

I hated being twenty-nine. Wasn't something important supposed to happen by thirty? What, exactly, had I been doing all these years?

"I should go to bed."

Quietly she said, "I'm glad you've come home."

"I can't stay long."

"I know that." She smiled her Mom-loves-you smile.

More than anything I wanted to tell her how scared I was. Instead, I said: "When did you start biting your nails?"

"Is it that noticeable?"

"Bloody cuticles, Mom. *Yeah*, kind of!"

She shrugged. I expected her to start bawling. But she got up, went to the fridge, opened it, then stood there for the longest time looking in. When she turned around finally she was holding a strawberry crème pie. "It's store-bought," she said. "I thought you'd like it."

I decided to take a piece and pretend to be very happy about it.

5: THE HOT SEAT

Mom and Dad had no insurance for a by-pass operation. Mark said he'd save for it. You bet he felt guilty because he worked for a big insurance company.

I felt guilty too. The least I could do was buy Dad a wheelchair. After three hours of arguing—"Make me happy," I told them. "*Indulge* me"—he and Mom agreed to let me.

I drove Dad to Visalia. It was overcast, the sky like an old mattress. The Valley would stay that way until spring. Only then would you see the bold purple silhouette of the Sierras. I'd been home three days.

When we got to Medical Supply and Therapy, a low whitewashed cinderblock building next to a used car lot, Dad refused to get out of the van.

"I called ahead," I said. "They've got wheelchairs."

He was slumped in the passenger seat. I hadn't turned off the engine, the radio tuned to old country. Bob wills was singing about the San Antonio Rose. Dad glowered out the window and said: "I can't go in a place like that."

"It's not a frigging funeral parlor, for Christsake."

"It's old," he said. "All the equipment's gonna be old. Forget it."

I let the van lurch away. Someone behind me leaned on the horn.

"Watch it!" Dad said. "Where you going in such a hurry?"

"Hell if I know."

"If this is too unpleasant for you, you can take me home."

"All I want to do is help," I said.

"You're helping."

"Not if you won't let me buy you a chair!"

"I'll only use it for a while," he said. "Save your money."

"They're not expensive. Not unless you want a motorized one."

"Now that would be depressing."

"All right," I said. "So let's get you a racy one with skinny bicycle tires."

He brightened, half his face rising. "I've seen those."

I pulled into the lot of Trekkers bicycle shop. As I helped Dad out, he leaned into me. I'd remembered him as small-boned but now there seemed to be a lot of him. Reeking of lemon-lime cologne, he was wearing his usual outfit, only today his sweatshirt was bright orange. It said in black block, "Exeter Gold."

Still gripping my arm, he gaped through the window at the racks of bikes. "They got chairs here?"

"Sure," I lied. I'd only wanted to get out of the van.

Our salesman was a tall guy with no whiskers, a sun-burnt nose, and sleek black hair pulled back in a ponytail. He gave me a look-over, his brown eyes pausing at the top of my hands, where a couple of tattoos came to an end: drumsticks.

Then he turned to my father: "Don't tell me, *hombre*. You want a tandem?"

"Actually," Dad said, "I want a submarine. You got one of those?"

Why do men feel compelled to joke like this?

When Mr. Tall played along, shaking his head in amuse-ment, his ponytail did a little dance. The lean lovely look of him made me wonder if I could handle a bike freak.

I told him what we needed.

He surprised me by saying: "We have one, *hermana*."

I wheeled Dad around in it, then he took a spin alone. Dad had good upper arm strength. Mr. Tall stood close by and watched. He said, "*Creo que es feliz.*"

I think he's happy.

"*Bastante,*" I said.

After we put the chair into the back of my van, he gave me his card. It said, *Alejandro Bikestand.*

"You can call me Ale," he said. Somehow he prevented himself from winking.

"Right," I said, "Ale Bikestand."

"*Claro!*"

Dad waved to him as I drove us away. "Nice boy," he said. "His eyes were all over you."

"Lucky me."

He glanced to the back. "Thanks for the bike, Rainy."

"It's a chair, Dad."

"I'm gonna call it a bike," he said.

6: PACKING HOUSE

Dad wheeled himself into the packing house. It was fridge-cool inside the barn-sized building. Noisy too, the conveyors rumbling. The graders were at one end, all of them women. Dad hadn't minded being among them. "You kidding?" he joked. "Me and all those white-gloved women?" They wore cotton gloves to protect their hands.

"It's a dying skill," he reminded me, as if he were giving a museum tour. Machines had taken over but weren't good enough yet to do the most careful sorting.

I hadn't been inside the House in several years. I'd for-gotten that the conveyors—where the graders stood—were raised nearly six feet above the concrete floor. That meant Dad couldn't get up there to surprise Mom.

"You want me to fetch her?" I asked.

He was peering up at them. "She can't leave the line."

Flushed-faced, no-necked Boo, Jr., the foreman, was am-bling our way. We had been in the same high school graduat-ing class. I didn't know he'd taken over his father's job.

He tipped his Oaks baseball cap at Dad. "Look at you, old man!"

Dad grinned his halfway grin. "Rainy bought me this bike."

Boo looked at me the way he'd always looked at me: like I was a mystery. I said, "Hey, Boo. Dad's training for a race."

"You back, Rainy?"

"Visiting."

"Convince her to stay, Boo."

He said to me, "You should stay."

"You need another packer, is that it?" I joked.

He glanced to the line above us. We were almost shout-ing to be heard. Then he looked again at me, his eyes as blue as a winter sky. "If your dad's not coming back, sure."

When I turned to see how Dad took this remark, he was pretending he hadn't heard. Mom noticed us finally. She tossed me an orange. It was an orchard run, the lowest grade.

"Watch it!" Boo called. He sounded irritated.

I said, "Lighten up, Boo."

He fixed his blues on me again: "You want a job, you come see me." Then he leaned down to squeeze Dad's shoulder. "You rest easy, old man."

The minute he was gone, Dad said, "Asshole."

Mom came down to join us. "I've got five minutes," she said. "Where'd you get the bike?" She pecked Dad on the forehead.

"It's a *chair*," I said.

"It's got bicycle tires," she said.

"That doesn't make it a bike."

"Will it hold up?" she asked. "It looks spindly."

"It's as light as excelsior," Dad said. He wheeled a small circle.

"Don't exert yourself."

"Mom, he's fine."

"I know he's fine."

"We just came by to say hello," I said. "Tonight I'm ordering us some take-out."

"To celebrate my racy bike," Dad said.

"Sure," I said. "And to send me off."

Mom frowned. "You're leaving already?"

"It's not like I'm moving to Alaska," I said.

"Mark will be here this weekend," Dad said.

"Kai's waiting," I said, "and I've got to get a gig."

"I thought you quit," Mom said.

"Didn't we agree it's a lousy business?" Dad added.

I laughed. A lousy business? There we were, shouting over the thrum and clatter of the belts, where Mom stood eight hours every day sorting oranges.

"I'll be back," I promised.

"For my funeral," Dad said glumly.

Mom and I looked at him abruptly. He waved us away, as if to say, *Stop it*. Mom was pale. I glanced to the tips of her gloves for pink stains. She said, "I've got work to do."

"And I've got wheelies to practice," Dad said.

Mom climbed up the steep steel steps. I stood there waiting for her to glance back and wave, but she kept on climbing and was gone. When I turned around, Dad was already yards away, wheeling for the door.

7: LAST SUPPER

"There's a good Cary Grant on tonight," Mom announced.

We were eating vegetarian Chinese on trays in front of the TV. "Alien III" was on cable. Watching horror movies was almost all Mom and Dad did when they were dating. Mom didn't know they gave Dad nightmares until after they were married. He'd wake up screaming.

"I can't watch black and white," Dad complained. "It gives me a headache."

"You grew up watching black and white," Mom said.

"Rainy, what do you think?"

"I want to see the Alien blown to a billion bits," I said. "But I don't want to wait for it."

Mom switched channels with the remote.

Wearing a white lab coat, Cary Grant stood on a scaffold next to an exhibit of a brontosaurus skeleton.

"Dinosaur's inaccurate," Dad said. "Tail shouldn't be dragging the ground."

"The movie was made, like, a hundred years ago," Mom said.

A bit of egg foo young slipped from the frozen side of Dad's mouth. Mom snatched it from the carpet and placed it on her paper plate.

"You got a good day for a drive tomorrow," he said. "No snow."

"We never get snow," I said.

When I was a girl, I resented this. The whitecaps of the bluish Sierras, twenty miles east, seemed a taunt. I imagined rich, childless couples skiing all day, then drinking hot coco around crackling fires. And laughing at us living in the Valley.

"If you stayed an extra day, you could see Mark," Mom said.

"I'll see him another time." I dreaded seeing Mark, he tried so hard to look happy. *Just come out*, I wanted to tell him. *It's okay.* But he was married now and *the manager of a division* and hopelessly over-invested in the dream Mom and Dad had never realized.

After Kate Hepburn made Cary Grant fall into the dinosaur skeleton, which collapsed in a heap, Dad said, "I could never live with someone like that."

"Lucky you got me," Mom said.

"Best grader on the line." He tried to wrinkle his nose at her but it didn't work.

Mom helped me clean up while Dad finished watching Alien III. She dumped the food into a single Tupperware container. "I like it mixed up," she said.

"Is Dad's wheelchair gonna be okay on the front porch?"

"This is Exeter," she said with a smart-aleck smile. "Not the *city*."

That night I dreamed of racing Dad in his wheelchair. I had one of my own. He was surprisingly fast, faster than me. When I was done, I slumped forward, gasping, my heart pounding in my head. Then I looked up and saw Dad far away, still wheeling fast. I wanted to call out to him but knew my voice wouldn't carry that far.

When I woke up, I was hoarse. Outside, the fog was so thick we couldn't see the houses across the street. "You can't go out there," Dad said. Seated in his "bike," he was turning circles in the living room—practicing.

Valley fog is the worst, responsible for pile-ups on the interstate every winter.

"If it's really bad, I'll come back," I said.

"What's wrong with your voice?" Mom asked suspiciously.

I was drinking her instant coffee. It didn't taste like coffee, but it felt good on my throat. I was hoping it'd give me a buzz.

Mom was frying cholesterol-free eggs. "Why bother if they aren't really eggs?" I asked.

"It's what your father likes," she said. "Sit down and eat something."

I poured a bowl of Cheerios and ate them dry. When I was seven I lived for nearly a year on nothing but cereal.

"I'm telling you, you're not going anywhere," Dad said.

"I hope that's not a comment on my career," I joked.

We were seated at the kitchen's tiny table.

Dad poured imitation maple syrup over his scrambled eggs. "A career is a *path*," he said. "At the end of that path you'll find—"

"The Wizard of Oz," Mom said. She sat down with a mug of coffee.

"I'm in the company of comedians," he said.

"*Comediennes*," I corrected.

"See how smart she is?" he said to Mom. Then to me: "You could go places, sweetie."

"Though today, apparently, I'm not going anywhere."

"You really shouldn't," Mom said.

"If it's really bad, I'll come back."

When I graduated from Exeter High, I'd won a scholarship to the College of the Sequoias, in Visalia. That's where my parents met. Neither graduated because Mom got pregnant with Mark. When I told them I wasn't going to Sequoia, they looked at me like I was speaking in tongues. "It just doesn't make sense," Dad said. For weeks he kept saying this.

Now I heard it again. "It doesn't make sense, your leaving in this fog."

I was in my van, the window rolled down, the fog so thick it was almost a drizzle. "I'll be back," I promised. I realized I kept saying this every time I saw them. Ten years earlier I had left in the same van, in almost the same way. It was eerie. Is this what children do, haunt their parents? Nearly everything I owned was in the van, my drums piled in the back. I needed my dog in the seat beside me: a forever-happy friend who's eager to go at a moment's notice. Maybe Kai was right. Nobody dreamed like this anymore. I was a cliché.

"You call us," Mom said.

Dad was shaking his head in dismay. I waved as I drove into the fog. They waved back, two oldish people with dwindling prospects and a daughter who couldn't leave them and their Valley fast enough. The fog was so thick I couldn't turn on my headlights. It worried me. I had to crawl out of there. It took hours. At one point I passed four cars raised up onto each other, like giant bugs caught humping. The ambulance's red strobe pulsed through the fog, reminding me of my own drumming heart. The fog didn't lift until I gained elevation at Altamont. That's where the wind farms are. Sleek, white windmills stand in rows that rise and fall with the hills, stretching miles across the sun-stunted grasslands. Kai said they're responsible for the deaths of more than a thousand eagles, hawks, and owls every year because they stand in a migratory flight path.

I didn't want to think about things like that, especially since it was clear nobody was going to take down the windmills. I imagined they made noise, those giant props, but not enough to warn the birds as they flew into them. Then I thought of the noisy turbines churning over the orange groves while my parents slept in their tiny house on their too-wide street and suddenly I wanted to turn around, as if I could warn them of the danger ahead.

ACKNOWLEDGMENTS

Stories in this collection first appeared as follows: "Winnemucca" in the *Chattahoochee Review* (finalist, Lamar York Fiction competition); "Boom, Like That!" in the *Greensboro Review* (winner, Pirate's Alley Faulkner Society gold medal); "Jackpot" in *The Quarterly* (Best of the West award); "Six Blind Cats" in *Mainstreet Rag*; "Far West" in Narrative Magazine (finalist, Narrative Magazine Competition; and "Story of the Week"); "Save the Poor Dumb Creatures" in *Turnstile*; "Tarzan (Again)" in *Green Mountain Review*; "Diversity" in *Crab Orchard Review* (winner, Jack Dyer Award); "Wheels" in *Gertrude Press* (winner, Gertrude Press chapbook competition).

I would like to thank Geoffrey Becker, Jessica Anya Blau, and Michael Downs for their love and insight; Luke Tennis for encouraging me to go west; Loyola University-Maryland for its ongoing support; and Jill Eicher for her abiding faith that her partner is worthy of the good that comes his way.

RON TANNER's writing has been named "notable" in both *Best American Essays* and *Best American Short Stories*. His awards for fiction include the G.S. Sharat Chandra Prize, the Jack Dyer Prize, the Charles Angoff Prize, the Faulkner Society gold medal, Pushcart Prize, New Letters Award, and many others, as well as fellowships from the Michener/Copernicus Society, Sewanee Writers Conference, and the National Park Service, to name a few. His novel *Missile Paradise* was named a "notable book of 2017" by the American Library Association. He lives on an historic farm in Maryland and directs the Good Contrivance Farm Writer's Retreat, an educational nonprofit.

ELIXIR PRESS TITLES

POETRY

Circassian Girl by Michelle Mitchell-Foust
Imago Mundi by Michelle Mitchell-Foust
Distance From Birth by Tracy Philpot
Original White Animals by Tracy Philpot
Flow Blue by Sarah Kennedy
A Witch's Dictionary by Sarah Kennedy
The Gold Thread by Sarah Kennedy
Rapture by Sarah Kennedy
Monster Zero by Jay Snodgrass
Drag by Duriel E. Harris
Running the Voodoo Down by Jim McGarrah
Assignation at Vanishing Point by Jane Satterfield
Her Familiars by Jane Satterfield
The Jewish Fake Book by Sima Rabinowitz
Recital by Samn Stockwell
Murder Ballads by Jake Adam York
Floating Girl (Angel of War) by Robert Randolph
Puritan Spectacle by Robert Strong
X-testaments by Karen Zealand
Keeping the Tigers Behind Us by Glenn J. Freeman
Bonneville by Jenny Mueller
State Park by Jenny Mueller
Cities of Flesh and the Dead by Diann Blakely
Green Ink Wings by Sherre Myers
Orange Reminds You of Listening by Kristin Abraham
In What I Have Done & What I Have Failed to Do by Joseph P. Wood
Bray by Paul Gibbons
The Halo Rule by Teresa Leo
Perpetual Care by Katie Cappello
The Raindrop's Gospel: The Trials of St. Jerome and St. Paula by Maurya Simon

Prelude to Air from Water by Sandy Florian
Let Me Open You a Swan by Deborah Bogen
Cargo by Kristin Kelly
Spit by Esther Lee
Rag & Bone by Kathryn Nuerenberger
Kingdom of Throat-stuck Luck by George Kalamaras
Mormon Boy by Seth Brady Tucker
Nostalgia for the Criminal Past by Kathleen Winter
I will not kick my friends by Kathleen Winter
Little Oblivion by Susan Allspaw
Quelled Communiqués by Chloe Joan Lopez
Stupor by David Ray Vance
Curio by John A. Nieves
The Rub by Ariana-Sophia Kartsonis
Visiting Indira Gandhi's Palmist by Kirun Kapur
Freaked by Liz Robbins
Looming by Jennifer Franklin
Flammable Matter by Jacob Victorine
Prayer Book of the Anxious by Josephine Yu
flicker by Lisa Bickmore
Sure Extinction by John Estes
Selected Proverbs by Michael Cryer
Rise and Fall of the Lesser Sun Gods by Bruce Bond
Barnburner by Erin Hoover
Live from the Mood Board by Candice Reffe
Deed by Justin Wymer
Somewhere to Go by Laurin Becker Macios
If We Had a Lemon We'd Throw It and Call That the Sun by Christopher Citro
White Chick by Nancy Keating
The Drowning House by John Sibley Williams

FICTION

How Things Break by Kerala Goodkin
Juju by Judy Moffat
Grass by Sean Aden Lovelace
Hymn of Ash by George Looney
Nine Ten Again by Phil Condon
Memory Sickness by Phong Nguyen
Troglodyte by Tracy DeBrincat

The Loss of All Lost Things by Amina Gautier
The Killer's Dog by Gary Fincke
Everyone Was There by Anthony Varallo
The Wolf Tone by Christy Stillwell
Tell Me, Signora by Ann Harleman
Far West by Ron Tanner